Sir Richard Meets His Match

Have faith,
Helene

Sir Richard Meets His Match

Helene Wallis

Eklund Publishers • Portland, CT

Copyright © 2024 Eklund Publishers,
A division of Eklund Media
All rights reserved.

Edited by: Kendra Plateroti

Cover photo by: Barbara Wallis
Cover design by: James Felgate

ISBN-13: 979-8-9898076-1-1

The characters and events portrayed in this book are fictitious. Any similarity to real persons, living or dead, is coincidental and not intended by the author.

No part of this book may be reproduced, or stored in a retrieval system, or transmitted in any form or by any means, electronic, mechanical, photocopying, recording, or otherwise, without express written permission of the publisher.

Printed in the United States of America

Acknowledgements

I wish to thank all of you who have encouraged me in writing this story.

I especially wish to thank Priscilla, Elisa, Laurie, and my daughter, Elizabeth Sampson, who spent hours reading and then giving me feedback on this book.

I also wish to thank my sons, Paul, David, Mark, James, and Daniel Felgate for their patience, as I tried to learn how to use a computer to write, correct, edit and then print out this manuscript, as they explained, over and over, how to do that. And then they opted to help me publish this book. Thank you so very much.

I also wish to thank my friends at The Atrium for their support and encouragement, as well as my many, many friends and acquaintances in the writing world, particularly members of the former Charter Oak Romance Writers (now re-grouped as Charter Oak Readers & Writers), for their support, suggestions and a gentle push and much encouragement when I needed it.

And to my life-long friends Amy Short Hnatko and Carla Ostergren Helfferich, and to my dear sister, Diane Wallis Jaquith, for always being there down through the years, often in the background, but also stepping up when I needed a word of encouragement or a push, to write my books.

And last of all to my editor Kendra Plateroti, who made excellent suggestions.

Thank you all.

God Bless,

Helene Wallis

Dedication

This book is dedicated to my parents, my grandmother and my great-grandmother, who all inspired in me a love of reading and writing.

My great-grandmother read to me for hours on end and taught me to read.

My grandmother inspired a love of writing, often citing her own published works.

My parents had, and read, a wide variety of books, magazines and newspapers, and encouraged my sister and I to read as well, by word and example.

I will love them and miss them forever.

Prologue

"They will hang me if I am caught" Jane said as she hurriedly hitched Dusty, her grey pony, to the cart. "Horse stealing is a hanging offense, but I can not leave you here."

Guiding the pony and cart down a little used track through the woods, Jane tried not to cry.

She looked over her shoulder every so often, but no one was following them... yet.

Chapter 1

"Are we really on the road?" she asked aloud. *As if a pony could talk.*

Dusty just twitched his ears.

The snow was coming down so thick and fast that Jane could not readily make out the track of the small lane she was traversing. She had dared not stay on the main roads because she had felt that they were sure to find her. The fact that the snow quickly obliterated the tracks from her little pony cart was reassuring.

She urged her sturdy grey pony on and clung to the reins as if they were a lifeline. *Where can I go and be safe?* The hedgerows to one side meant that she could not even hide among them if anyone happened along the little lane. She laughed to herself. The tracks would give them away. *Who would come along today? Who would be out in this storm?* Everyone would be home snug before the fire. *Everyone, but the men searching for me. Everyone else but me, for I no longer have a home.* And the tears flowed afresh.

Christmas is coming and no treat for Dusty this year. Another Christmas and no family for me. The tears flowed faster and formed crystals on her cheeks.

Looking closely at the curvature of the terrain Jane noted that it swung to the left. *That must be the way the lane goes* she thought as she signaled Dusty to the left.

Moments later, the cart lurched and then they were landing with a splash in the gurgling frigid water. The cart tipped over, the pony thrashing to free itself and Jane, barely conscious, lying draped over the top of a large ice encrusted rock, the cart upside down on top of her, her face just a hair's breadth from the gurgling water.

I am going to drown, Jane thought as she tried to keep her head above the rushing, icy water. She opened her mouth to scream as some water took advantage and rushed in. She spit it out quickly and took a deep breath. Terror gripped her and in that moment she found that she was more afraid of drowning than she was of the men pursuing her; more afraid of drowning than hanging.

Jane tried to move and found she had completely lost feeling in her limbs. Numbness spread through them as she tried desperately to free herself. It was as if a giant hand were holding her down. Panicky, she tried to kick but her legs refused to move. She could not see; her eyelids were frozen shut.

She was cold, so cold. Her teeth chattered noisily like castanets. *Would I be better off drowning than hanging*? She thought moments before she lost the battle and then lost consciousness as her head dropped downwards toward the deadly depths of the stream.

The sound of hooves crunching through the snow nearby went unheard by the now unconscious Jane.

Chapter 2

"Bloody hell!" Sir Richard Winslow exclaimed as he saw a cart partially submerged in the small brook that ran alongside the southernmost end of his property. A ride to erase the cobwebs from his mind had brought him to what was clearly a tragedy for he doubted the driver of the small cart had survived. The pony, meanwhile, had partially freed itself from its harness and was struggling against the straps.

After wading into the bubbling icy brook, he tugged on the cart with all of his might in an effort to pull it off of its sure-to-be-deceased driver. It would not budge.

He could not, in good conscience, leave it there while he rode for help. There was always the slightest chance that the poor sod was not dead. The time it took to get help would surely doom the boy so he braced himself at the other side and pushed as hard as he could and was rewarded with the sound of a moan as he felt the cart shift. *Ah, the fellow is alive*!

He renewed his efforts and the cart shifted enough that he could rest part of its side on a partially exposed rock and then, getting down on his knees in the frigid water, reached under and pulled the victim by his cloak.

Her cloak. The driver was a woman. Sensible to a woman's wants, for he had two sisters, his parents had given up on the quest for a spare with the second girl, he felt around for her reticle. Nothing. One last grab, for the girl was unconscious and he was now feeling like the proverbial block of ice himself, Sir Richard found himself clutching a leather pouch and he hauled that out and with much difficulty pulled the young woman from the brook and dragged her up the slight slope to his waiting horse. *Now, how to get a dead weight up on a horse. And ride too?*

Then, freeing the pony from the last of its traces, he noted that it was sturdy and aside from scratches and some small cuts, was able to walk normally and was docile.

It might be romantic in a Mrs. Radcliffe novel, he thought, remembering his sisters' enjoyment of such rot, but in real life this would not work. Straining, even though she was quite slender, he finally managed to get her slung over the back of the pony. Dripping water was sluicing off of her garments and the snow was still coming thick and fast. Her long, brown hair was plaited in a single braid and her boots were shabby and well worn.

Holding the long reins of the pony he swung up onto the saddle of his bay gelding, Roman.

Shivering violently, he realized they could well die of exposure out there if he did not get back to the Hall in short order. Leading the pony by the reins, he set out on what might be his last ride, he reflected, as he was so numb, he no longer felt cold and he could not even tell if his feet were in the stirrups, though he believed that they were...

Stay awake. Stay awake. He was nearly chanting in his quest to stay upright in the saddle as they rode towards the Hall.

I will not make it, he realized. The shortest route to the barn was not the wisest route for there was no chance he would find anyone to help them on the way and it was much too far for him in this condition. He reluctantly directed the horse to a small cabin just a short way along.

Jane's teeth were chattering violently when she awoke to find herself hanging upside down on the side of a horse. *I am being kidnapped* was her first thought.

No, that was ridiculous, *who would kidnap an orphan with only a pony and cart for possessions*, and she was lucky to have that. The cart and the pony would have been taken and she would have been left at the side of the lane. *At least I think that we had been on a lane*. The snow was so thick that she had followed the lay of the land and remembered, hazily, the cart tipping.

I must have landed in water, she thought, for she was thoroughly soaked and shaking violently from the cold.

Chapter 3

No time to reach the village, either, Sir Richard thought, as they neared the cottage in the woods that his sisters and he had played in as children. A one room cabin, it had provisions and warm blankets.

He still went there when he wanted privacy, for there was little of that at the Hall, as large a structure as it was.

Even his sisters used the cabin, especially in the summer, so there might be some extra women's clothing there as well. He hoped that there were warm items for he had never paid attention to whatever his sisters had hanging in the corner wardrobe. He did know that they had extra shifts there, for they liked to swim in the little pond in their shifts.

No time now to care for the cattle. He dismounted, trudged through the deepening snow, opened the door to the cottage, propped it open and threw more kindling on the logs in the fireplace. Using a piece of flint, he started a fire and then went out to bring in the girl.

She wriggled when he pulled her down from the pony and he saw her put out a hand in an attempt to keep herself upright, although her eyes were closed.

"Where are we going?" the girl asked through chattering teeth.

Her voice was faint, hoarse.

Sir Richard quietly explained that he was trying to get her into a place where she could get warm. He also said "You will be safe here" as he thought she would naturally be frightened. After all, they had never met.

Bad luck if she casts up her accounts, he thought as he put one of her arms over his shoulder and attempted to walk her those few steps to the cottage.

They did not speak, but she made a valiant effort to stay upright. He could not help but admire her courage as she tried to walk next to him before collapsing at the door of the cottage, ending up in a heap on the doorstep. Now, how was he to get her up the step and into the cottage? He could feel a faint promise of heat from the fire, already slightly warming the air. It was so cold that zero would feel warm, he thought, as he tried to lift her up again.

She shook her head, so he let go and stepped back. She then slowly crawled inside through the doorway. Sir Richard smiled to himself. What pluck! Following her inside, for she had managed to get through the doorway before again collapsing, he strode to a chest and pulled out blankets and rolling her on to it, dragged her to the fireplace. She opened her eyes. *Light*, he noted absently, blue or maybe hazel. He instructed her to get herself out of her clothing, dry herself with a piece of toweling he gave her, and to wrap herself in a blanket.

Following his own advice, he stripped off his clothing and proceeded to briskly rub his body with a piece of toweling, and wrapping the blanket around himself, in deference to her maiden sensibilities, he rummaged through a dresser along the wall for clothing that he could put on.

After he had put on trousers and a shirt, he went to find boots. He knew he had a spare pair in the corner and turned them over to make sure no mice were cowering inside. That had happened in the past (much to the amusement of his sisters when he had gotten his boots wet as a child and put his foot into one in which a mouse had taken up residence.) He put the boots on and turned to see the girl lying there on the blanket with her mouth open.

Oh, no doubt she had never seen a naked man before. *Well, too late for the niceties, this is life or death here*, he thought as he pointed to the blanket and said, "If you do not wish to freeze to death, you will get out of those wet garments and wrap yourself in a blanket."

Taking two more wool blankets outside, he rubbed down the horse and the pony and put them in the adjoining lean-to with some hay. He would bring some water after he had melted some snow over the fire in the cottage fireplace. It was crowded with both the horse and the pony in there, but their combined body heat would keep each of them warm enough, Sir Richard reasoned, and he returned to the cottage.

The girl was lying wrapped in the blanket in front of the fire. He saw tears on her cheeks.

Is she crying? No, she had been crying for she was no longer awake. She was still dressed in her wet garments. He called "Miss? Miss?"

She opened her eyes then. Pretty blue eyes looked up at him. "You need to get out of that wet dress, my dear." he said but she just shook her head.

Puzzled, he studied her for a moment. Her face was composed although her teeth were chattering.

"Why have you not..." he started to ask when she said just one word. "Buttons."

SIR RICHARD MEETS HIS MATCH

This would not be the first woman he had undressed, he thought, as he tried to unbutton the buttons that marched down the front of her simple day dress. The dress was stiff and icy, the buttons unyielding. "I will purchase you a new dress" he muttered as he put his hands at the front of the neckline and using his knife cut it down the entire length as she cried out in surprise, and most likely, embarrassment. He pulled it from her, with her trying to clutch it to her body. Winning the tussle, he tossed the cloth aside.

"You...you," she sputtered, apparently unable to think of what to say next, as he then ripped off her chemise and then her drawers and started to pat her skin gently dry with a piece of toweling. She tried to stop him, as she clutched the remnants of her chemise to herself, in an effort to cover her body.

"I have two sisters, you know," he said quietly as he dried her back, "I taught them how to swim in their chemises. They were unhappy with me after I threw them into the water, for they were more or less naked for all that, but I know that they will never drown if they are in the water for any reason. So, there is no mystery to me about a woman's body."

He hoped that would make her feel more at ease as he loosely placed a blanket around her shivering form and tugged the sodden, icy chemise from her hands.

No point in mentioning to her about the few mistresses he had had in the past.

He knew his way around a woman's body and hers was perfection, from all he had seen. He wanted her to feel comfortable and to trust him. So, he did not ogle her body and forced himself to be all business while he helped tuck the blanket close around her.

She was still cold, and her teeth were chattering, and she was very drowsy. Too drowsy. He studied her. *What would Nurse do?*

He thought back to when he was still a young lad and had come into the nursery half frozen one time after he had fallen into the pond after breaking through thin ice. Nurse had put him in to a warm bath. 'Not too hot' she had said 'for you can get burned that way.'

That is what I have to do, he thought, and grabbing a bucket he went out to bring in more snow and soon had a large kettle of snow melting over the fire. After the water was warm, but not hot, he pulled out a slipper tub he had brought there for the benefit of his sisters who liked to wash off the brook water, even though he had tried to point out that the water that they were bathing in came from the brook. His mother had stopped him just in time.

"Do you want to haul water all the way there from the well all the way from the Hall?" Well, no, he certainly did not. "Then say nothing', she advised him. Obviously, she was not planning on having the servants do it.

That little tub is coming in handy now, he thought, as he started pouring in buckets of water.

Rummaging through the dresser he even found some scented soap that one of his sisters had left behind and that evidently the mice did not care for and one last dry towel. Once the tub was half full of water, not too warm but warm enough, he hoped, he went to where the girl was lying, asleep in front of the fire, then unwrapped her from the blanket and carried her naked form to the He tried to wake her up by talking to her but she just shook her head in her sleep and refused to open her eyes.

There was nothing for it but to lower her into the tub, splashing water on himself as he tried to maneuver her gently down into it. *Well, that did not go well he thought*, as he found himself fairly wet in the bargain, for he was unprepared when she started thrashing about.

The girl woke up with a start and started to fight him.

He spoke gently to her, and she finally relaxed and seemed to drowse off again. *Poor girl. I wonder where she came from. She is not from around here.* He washed her gently but did not dare try to wash her hair. He had no idea how he would be able to rinse it and tried to keep her plaited braid of dark brown hair out of the tub. That did not work either. Well, it would dry eventually he was sure and decided to ignore it.

Her teeth stopped chattering after a few moments and her skin turned rosy in color but not too red. She felt warmer now, not like a block of icy meat. A bad analogy but there it was, the facts. He liked facts. Usually. He did not think she would like his description of how she had felt in his arms and vowed to himself never to utter those words out loud.

He gently, for the second time, dried her body and helped her, and well, dressed her, for she was little help, in a sleep shift one of his sisters left there at the cottage last summer. It was not terribly warm, but it would serve to help her keep her modesty, although he had seen and touched her entire body. Then he took the blanket from the single bed there and wrapped it around her.

Chapter 4

The last thing Jane remembered was when she was driving the cart. She must have gotten wet somehow. It felt like she was encased in ice.

She was also lying in the doorway of what looked like a small cabin with a strange man. He was trying to drag her through the doorway.

She looked up at him and shook her head, so he let go and stepped back. She might be mortified to be found in this position, helpless with a dress that was molded to her body by the water like a corset made of ice, but she was also practical. *I need to get in where it is warm.* She tried to crawl because she knew she could not stand. She was too weak, too cold, and too scared. *Who IS he? How did I get here? Where is Dusty? Am I in danger from him?*

The strange man then had stripped off his clothing and calmly dressed in dry clothes. Apparently, his clothing had gotten wet too.

Jane did not know what to say. She had had a strange man strip her naked, bathe her like a child and then dry her naked body and now here she was, dressed in a night rail, sitting in front of a roaring fire, finally beginning to feel somewhat warm, although she was still shivering a little and her teeth continued to chatter at intervals. The wool blanket that was wrapped around her was of finely spun wool. No doubt the man raised sheep. She had seen a few sheep farms in the area during her flight. *Mayhap he is a sheep farmer.*

She felt odd thanking him; after all, he had stripped her bare. However, she knew he had saved her life and that was what counted. He had not said a word out of place. In fact, he had said very little. A taciturn man then. Like her father. Looking over her shoulder as the man rummaged in a dresser she said, "Thank you for saving my life. I owe you a debt."

The man stopped and turned and looked at her with a steady gaze. Brown eyes, she thought, and a pleasant face but not one that smiled a lot. A quiet, steady kind of man. Hopefully, a good man.

The man nodded his head and then said, quietly, "You needed rescuing, Miss, and I just happened to come along in time to rescue you. You nigh on drowned back there."

After a moment, she nodded. Now, with the realization that if she had not drowned, she would have frozen to death out there.

He continued "People have helped me out when I needed it." He spoke in a quiet, thoughtful tone of voice, "and you will repay me down the road, I do not doubt, by helping out someone else in need." The man then turned back to the dresser and started to pull out clothing.

From the looks of it he had found some chemises. He threw them at Jane and without noting her reaction went to a cupboard and looked through some items hanging on hooks and then took out a few simple dresses that looked like it might be of a size to fit her. "I have sisters. They like to come here to get away, too," he said by way of explanation when he saw the startled look on her face while handing her women's clothing in several different sizes. "You can wear one of these tomorrow. For tonight stay in the night wear. I am putting you to bed right after supper is served. You can choose what fits you for tomorrow when we leave here if the weather is improved."

Looking up at him, she realized that she had not thought beyond right now. Tomorrow will come and she would be on her way if the cart and her pony were in good shape. Good God: she had not even thought to ask about Dusty. She opened her mouth to ask but before the words were out, he was speaking.

"I will tend to the cattle," he said, and quit the now warm room. *He said cattle, so Dusty might be here too.*

Jane looked through the clothing. There were some chemises, fine wool stockings, and four wool day dresses, in two different sizes. She chose a dress that looked closest to her size, plus a chemise, and stockings before he returned.

"The weather has turned even nastier, so I think we are here for a spell," he said as he threw more wood on the fire, after stomping some snow off of his boots at the doorway.

As he removed his gloves and shrugged out of his coat, Jane took a good look at the man who had saved her life. He was tall and though perhaps not handsome, he was good enough looking for any young lady's tastes, as well as being a kind and competent man. His hair was brown and cut a little longer than she was accustomed to seeing.

"So, we will have to spend, the, uh, night here?" she asked because she could only see one bed in the room, along with the table, two dressers, a cupboard, a supply of wood, four chairs, and an armchair that looked very comfortable. She wanted to curl up in it with a book. *Look at me, being very fanciful.* But it was true. It was the perfect place to spend an evening with a few candles lit, a fire in the fireplace, a dog or cat by the hearth, and a good book.

Chapter 5

The Lord save him, he almost laughed out loud. She wanted to know if they were staying the night here, *where else.* Common sense stopped him from uttering the words out loud. She has been through an ordeal and handled it better than some of the debutantes he had met at *ton* events. *And she is young and very innocent at a guess.*

"That is a good possibility" he answered, and stirred the wood and added another small log. He would have to bring in more wood if they were staying for any length of time. "In the meantime, I will make us a meal, you must be hungry. When is the last time you ate food?" he asked her, for he had heard her stomach rumble long before he had stripped her naked.

"Yesterday morning," she had answered after a moment of thought.

"Yesterday?" Morning?" he asked. A runaway, then. There was no other explanation. She was not from around here. He knew everyone in these parts. No point in asking her where she came from. He would not get a straight answer.

"Where are you going?" he asked, although he could guess the answer.

"London" she said, quietly.

"Where were you going in London?"
"To an employment agency."
"What are your skills?"
"Skills?"
"What did you plan to do for work?"
She hesitated before answering "Oh, uh, a governess I think."
"Do you have references?"
"References? Uh, no. But I love children."
"You will not find gainful employment without references. I can write to your former employers for references for you. I will have my man of business take care of that after you give me the particulars."
"Oh, no. No. I can not."
"My dear, the only employment I can see for you without you starving in the stews is on your back, if I may speak plainly. You will need references."
What kind of work is that?" she asked, clearly not understanding.

"As a whore" he blurted out as he had been getting tired of her not being forthright with him. He almost smacked himself in the forehead when he realized that she was far more innocent than he had realized as she blushed so deep a red that even in the dimness of the cottage he could see. Tears came to her eyes.

Too late to take those words back. "Is the pony yours?" he asked, in as gentle a tone of voice as he could manage.

"Yes, Papa gave me Dusty for a gift, but no one believes he is mine" she said, wiping a tear from her eye.

"And the cart?"

"I, uh, borrowed it" she said in a quiet, toneless voice. "He is too small for me to ride. Or, rather, I have gotten too big," she said with a small smile, tears again sparkling on her cheeks.

So, he is harboring a thief. It was not difficult to guess what had happened.

"Your parents died?" he asked, gently.

"A carriage accident, in fact," she said, perhaps seeing the twisted humor in that she had had a similar difficulty and nearly the same fate.

"Recently?"

"No, but they came yesterday to take everything away, including Dusty," she said, the tears now coursing down her cheeks, as she furiously tried to dab at them with the edge of the blanket.

"So, you ran away."

"I told them I was going to the barn to say good-bye to Dusty, and they laughed at me" she said, and the tears streamed down her face in earnest. "So, I, uh, borrowed the cart and left through the woods."

"Where did you sleep last night?"

"In the woods just off the main road, and, and they came looking for me, but I was already well hidden. I saw them ride by and then later they came back," she said and hiccupped. "So, I left the road and took a small lane. Then it snowed. I, I must have lost the path in the snow."

The whole time Richard was leaning against the frame of the closed door, thinking. It was a tale that was repeated time after time. The father dies and the family gets turned out to live with relatives or the best they can. As for Dusty, everything reverts back to the estate. So Dusty was no longer hers. "I can help you," he said before he thought.

She blinked.

He wondered what made him say that. That is not what he meant to say when he had opened his mouth. *Yet, why not*? He could help her, and it would not hurt him at all. He thought on it. I have more than enough blunt to live on, even with two sisters to dower and launch in London starting next year. My estate is profitable. I have a very comfortable living. The problem for me is when my sisters begin their come outs and I have to find a wife.

Next year he would be heading to London with his mother and sisters. He was not looking forward to the whole situation. Nothing felt as distasteful as looking over women like cattle at a horse market and selecting a brood mare to bring home. There should be a better way to choose a wife. He had need of a wife and that is how it is done. He mentally shrugged.

On the other hand, his eldest sister has been waxing on and on about the splendors of the Season and all of the men she thought would fall at her feet. Although she is pretty enough to take, Richard knew that the fortune hunters would be lined up with hands out, vying for her dowry. "Just give me the direction of the solicitors and I will contact them. We will leave here in the morning, and I will send word to them that you and, uh, Dusty, are here."

He put the ingredients for porridge in the pot and another for water and swung them both into the fireplace and then went to get his outdoor clothing.

The girl walked over to the fireplace and held her hands out, clearly enjoying the warmth of the flames. Tears were still running down her face. *I will never understand women,* he thought as he pulled on his still wet boots and shrugged on his still sodden wet coat and picked up a bucket of water that he had gotten by melting snow.

He opened the door and peered out. Night had fallen and it was still snowing. The horse and pony were settled in the lean-to. He wanted to make a last check on them, give them some water and then bring in some more firewood. *It is going to be a long night.*

He called over his shoulder just before he went through the door, "Make yourself at home and I will return after I have checked the cattle."

He saw the girl turn from the fireplace and make for the table. He slipped out of the door and shards of ice from his wet clothing seemed to stab him. He sucked in a quick breath and hastened to finish his tasks so he could return to the warmth of the cabin.

He made it quick, for he was hungry and cold. Stepping into the cabin, he stripped off his wet garments. It felt good to be back inside the cabin again, the roaring fire had significantly warmed the air.

He removed his still wet boots and put them near the fireplace, put on a dry warm shirt, and then he heaped bowls with steaming porridge and sugar. "I am sorry there is not milk for the porridge, but I have honey here," he said to her as placed the bowl in front of her at the table. He poured mugs of coffee and placed them on the table as well. "I am sorry that we are all out of tea."

She just shook her head and stirred some sugar into the coffee. He bowed his head to say grace and she followed suit.

'We', why had he just said 'when we leave'? Jane was asking herself, as she held the warm cup of coffee in her hands. *Is he really going to send Dusty and the cart back? How am I to repay him for saving my life? In his bed? Could I have fallen into another nightmare?* Tears were running down her face. *I am homeless. Penniless. Helpless. I have no way to repay his kindness, if it is kindness. Does he expect me to be his mistress*

now? For rescuing me? Will he send me back to hang? Would I have been better off drowning?

Jane was touched that after thanking God for their health, food and shelter, he asked that her parents please rest in peace. She found herself tearing up a little again. *He is a good man,* she thought as she tasted the first bit of her porridge, *at least I think he is.*

Looking up at his face she said, "I do not even know your name."

He laughed, his mouth smiling and his eyes crinkling in amusement. "And I do not know yours."

They spent the rest of the mealtime talking about their families.

He had even had some dealings with the cousin of her mother who had had her turned out of her home.

"He always seemed like a fair man" was his only comment on the cousin.

Jane enjoyed herself and soon found herself starting to doze.

When suggested she go to bed, she climbed into the bed and put her head on the pillow.

Jane awoke. She was warm, comfortable, and for the first time in two days she was not hungry, and cold, and afraid. There was a mound of something nice and warm against her back. She rolled on to her back and flung her arm out, her eyes still closed. Her questing hand rested on warm flesh.

She opened her eyes. *Oh, no.* She then remembered. *I am in a bed. With a man*! Turning her head and looking over she could see that he was awake and looking at her, an amused smile on his face. And from the little she could see and feel with her body, feet and legs, he was as naked as sin. And, from the nudging she had felt on her back while on her side, he was aroused. At least that was as good a guess as an innocent woman could make. Not that she was going to ask him.

"I am going to get out of bed now," he said with the hint of laughter in his voice. You might want to close your eyes to keep from a virginal faint, or not. Your choice," he said as he was reaching over her for articles of clothing that were neatly folded on a chair next to the bed, his arm brushing her now very sensitive feeling breast. *Why so tender?*

Jane was dressed in a fine linen nightgown. She did not remember donning it. Her last memory was of him bathing her in the tub as if she was a baby. Then she remembered eating porridge at the table.

Blushing beet red (she felt her skin turning hot, in fact), she closed her eyes tightly as he climbed over her, put the blanket back over her, tucked it in.

Then she remembered. He had given her the nightgown and instructed her to put it on. She had tried to put it on herself but could not, she was still so cold, and he had bathed her naked body and then had dressed her in it. Before turning in he had banked the fire for the night and bade her to go to bed. Then he had told Jane to close her eyes if she was feeling shy and then Sir Richard had shed his clothing and climbed into the bed, positioned himself at the wall for that is the coldest part of the bed, he had informed her, and he had promptly fallen asleep.

She had lain awake for some time quietly weeping in sorrow for her situation. She had had little time to properly mourn losing the only home she had ever known. Then she said her prayers, including thanks for being rescued. She had to admit that Sir Richard is a kind man. *I feel safe with him, even though we are sharing a bed. After all, if he had designs on me, he would have done something by now. What he would have done? No one had ever explained what happens in a bed when with a man, but something should have happened by now, right? Although I have a basic idea,* she thought, for she had watched dogs coupling although she was sure it was somewhat different for people.

Now it is morning, I hope he will help me. How will I ever repay him? Opening her eyes, she watched him leaning over to put on more wood and stoke the ashes until he had a good-sized fire going. As he turned away from the fireplace, she closed her eyes as Sir Richard dressed swiftly, the image of his body- his mostly naked body, at least from the back- firmly fixed in her brain.

Chapter 6

After he put a kettle of water in the fireplace to heat, Richard put on his boots and coat and went out to take care of the horse and pony. It was lightly snowing. Judging by the snow now falling, they might have to stay one more night. If he had a sleigh at the cabin, then they would have no problems leaving.

Good thing there were plenty of provisions in the cottage.

He needed to melt more snow for water, however. Using a pail he had brought from the cottage, he brought in some snow and stomping on the outside threshold to get as much snow off of his boots as possible, he entered the cottage.

The girl had changed into the day dress he had given her yesterday. Her long brown hair, almost black in color, was still hanging in a plait down her back. Jane was stirring something in the pot. Looking around, he could see that the bed was made, and the nightgown was folded neatly on a chair.

"Where did you learn to cook over a fire, Miss Smith?" he asked her.

She turned and smiled. "My papa taught me long ago." Silence reigned for a few minutes.

Moments later she was ladling out porridge into two bowls.

He collected spoons from the dresser that served as the kitchen as she placed the food and two mugs of coffee on the table and sat in one of the chairs.

Chapter 7

Jane did not know what to talk about. Should she ask him if she is now his prisoner, or if he intended to keep her as his mistress? Although, *if he wanted me as a mistress, he surely would have done so last night, would he not?*

Maybe he thinks I am too plain for that? Then, *am I to feel insulted he does not think I am good enough to be a mistress?* She bit back a smile at such a ridiculous thought.

How will I get to London or any city with no cart? I can not ride Dusty and I certainly can not walk to the next large city. Whatever will happen to me? Will he turn me out when he finds I am unable to repay him? Surely, he is expecting some coin.

Sir Richard had been watching her face. *What is she thinking? Well, time to talk about their situation. She is ruined if this gets about*, he thought.

He tasted the oatmeal. "This is very good, um, Miss Smith" he said.

"Thank you, uh, Sir Richard," she answered.

"I know it is not proper, but you may as well call me Richard while we are private" he said. "After all, we have shared a bed," he said with an easy smile.

"Whatever are we to do?" she asked. "I need to know. The suspense about my future is eating me alive."

"When we return to the world, you will know me as Sir Richard Winslow," he said and winked at her.

"I am no one, but my father is-was-a noted scholar and studied antiquities. I, uh, helped him with his writing and even with his field work."

"Hence your skills cooking over a fire" he said and smiled. "It sounds like you are-were leading an interesting life."

"Oh, yes, helping Papa was such, a. uh, a" and the tears began.

"I am sorry, Sweeting, uh, Miss Smith, I have not even offered my condolences on the passing of your parents. I am sorry. Such a shock and then to be turned out so callously. I am sorry, my dear."

The tears were falling now, and he watched as she drew herself upright, wiped her face and attempted to smile. His sisters had turned into watering pots when they had all lost their father, but, they had never had to deal with all that this young woman had to handle. He felt admiration for this brave young woman and vowed to himself to help her as much as he could.

"We may have to spend another night, Miss Smith" he said. "It is difficult to know. The snow is coming down lightly. When I feed the cattle later, I will see if the storm seems to be dying. I am not sure riding double on my horse is a good idea with falling snow."

"Thank you, Sir, uh, Richard. I will be on my way as soon as may be."

"Do you really plan to go all the way to London? You might get something for the necklace and earbobs, they are of good quality, but not enough to take care of you and your pony the entire way and then find lodgings in London."

"You found my jewelry? Oh, no, I do not plan to sell them. They were my mothers. I had to sneak them out, too."

"Were they listed on the property sheets?" He had to know for he would pay for them, too, if they were.

"She had given them to me on my majority and no one saw them. I took them out of my dresser first thing and put them in the leather pouch and hid it in the straw, in Dusty's stall," she said as he got up from his chair and went over to another dresser where he had the pouch wrapped in a towel. He brought it over to her.

She took out the pearl necklace and earbobs and smiled.

"After the snow stops and the weather clears, we will depart for the Hall. Weatherby Hall is ancient but has been modernized for comfort."

"I, I do not know if, that is…"

"You will go to Weatherby Hall, Miss Smith, and I will contact my solicitor and man of business. You will stay as my guest until everything is concluded. Do I make myself clear?"

"Yes, very clear," she answered him, as there was no other recourse. *She has no other choice*, he thought.

"I, uh, Sir, uh, Richard, I have no idea how to go on."

"You can help me." *When did I get that idea?* Richard found himself now wondering for that is not what he had been thinking of just moments ago.

"How may I help you, Sir Richard?"

"I collect old coins. I have some Roman ones I found not too long ago that I have not had a chance to research. You, could, uh, help me."

"You are interested in antiquities too, Sir Richard?"

"In a manner of speaking."

"I do not understand," she said, a puzzled expression on her face.

"It is a new hobby of sorts. I found a coin recently and was excited about it and put it in my office. Then I found another one and the next thing I knew I was looking for more. I am planning on finding out more about old coins in London next year."

"I know about old coins. Papa has, had, some old coins. He was more interested in pottery. I like the coins."

"You like old coins?" Richard asked, not believing his good luck.

Richard was digesting this conversation as they continued to eat breakfast and sip coffee when the jingle of harness was faintly heard. *No, not harness. Sleigh bells. Bloody Hell. No doubt his sisters and mother were on the way to rescue him and bear him off to the Church service in the village. Yes, today is Sunday. Nothing keeps mama from Church on Sunday.*

Doubtless the squire would be with them as he had been quietly courting his mother for months and often picked them up in his carriage for Church on Sunday mornings.

What to do with Miss Smith? She can be left alone here at the cottage. How to explain the pony? They would come in no doubt. No place to hide her. Not that I am the kind of man to hide a problem. She is ruined. Only one thing to do.

Richard quickly rose to his feet. *I have to do this before they reach here and she knows what is happening.* He walked around the table until he was standing next to her.

He took her hand in his as she looked warily up at him. *She knows me too well. That might be a good thing, or it might not,* he found himself thinking.

"Miss Smith, I know it is short notice but will you, uh, marry me? "

Chapter 8

Sir Richard was fiddling with his fingers, Jane noted. Something he did when he was thinking. She had noticed it last night but had not registered its significance.

Jane was enjoying this little breakfast, even if there was no clotted cream and no hot chocolate when she awoke this morning. *Sir Richard is congenial and easy to talk to.* She watched his face as he recounted an episode involving his sisters one summer when they were all young.

And then wonder of wonders, the subject changed to Roman coins and Jane grew excited to be able to talk about one of her favorite subjects.

Jane could not believe it. *Sir Richard is interested in coins, too. And he needs someone to help him. I can do that. I can repay him for his generosity by helping him build a coin collection. I must know as many places to look for coins as anyone else. Mayhap he will let me stay here in this cottage for now. No one will know I am here contact anyone on my behalf. I will be safe.*

I just want to hug him. I am not going to be a burden to Sir Richard. I will not have to beggar myself in London and starve on the way there. I will not have to prostitute myself to survive, though I have no idea how anyone goes about that, either. Oh, this is wonderful!

She smiled widely and caught an arrested expression on Sir Richard's face. *Does he think I am ugly? Oh, what does that matter? It is not as if he wants to marry me or has to even. No one knows we are here alone together.*

Suddenly Sir Richard rose to his feet and stopped right next to her and took her hand in his and looked down at her. *His face is solemn looking, serious. I wonder what the problem is?*

Something is afoot. First Sir Richard was sitting perfectly still as if in deep thought and now he is holding my hand and asking me to marry him. I do not understand why. Oh dear...

"I am honored by your unexpected proposal, Sir Richard, but I am not sure we will suit." Jane said and smiled up at him. *Such a nice man. A true gentleman...*

Sir Richard spoke then. "My dear, you can cast me aside later on, but as far as the world knows, you are my intended bride," and at that the door burst open and four people invaded what had been their private oasis as he slipped a ring on the third finger of her left hand.

Chapter 9

"Oh, Dear" Jane heard from an elegant lady as the greetings were shouted out by those accompanying her, before anyone had taken in the scene before them. The woman was holding on to the arm of a man of means as evidenced by the tailoring of his clothing and his highly polished boots. They were closely followed by two young ladies who now stood there with mouths agape and staring eyes…

Jane felt Sir Richard give her hand a gentle squeeze and then letting go of her hand she watched him walk across the floor to embrace the elegant woman, shake the hand of the wealthy gentleman, and then hug each of the young ladies in turn. The young ladies were clearly shocked. No doubt the man and woman were also but were much too polite to show more than mere interest.

There were two young ladies and very nicely dressed in bonnets with just enough trim to be decorative but not so much as to be over the top. They wore cloaks of fine wool and carried white rabbit fur muffs. Their half boots were very fashionable. Jane felt absolutely dowdy in comparison when she considered her shabby cloak and plain bonnet that was now misshapen from its dunking in the water.

Jane wanted to hide. Here she sat, a now fallen woman. *No one will want to hire me now. What will I do? Will he purchase Dusty and the cart for me? Now I will not ever get a position as a governess or even a companion. I am ruined beyond redemption.* She then looked down at the ring on her finger, much too large, of course, but there it was, a signet ring. His ring.

Clasping her hands together, Jane pasted a smile of welcome on her face. No doubt it looks like a grimace, she was thinking, as Sir Richard turned and started walking towards her. Then, with his back to the others, he winked, and she knew, just knew, *everything is going to be all right.* Somehow.

"Mum, Mr. Howard, girls. May I present to you my fiancé, Miss Jane Smith," and literally hauling her to her feet he whispered, "play along, or-else."

Jane, with a bad feeling about what the 'or else' could mean, smiled a brittle smile and was immediately embraced by the woman, who said "I am surprised but pleased that my son has chosen a wife. I am sure we will become fast friends, my dear. Welcome to the family."

Jane felt herself blush for she would never be part of the family, though it felt like it could be something wonderful. She felt terrible for not instantly denouncing this betrothal. *I feel like such a beast for defrauding this family.* Before she could even blink, her hand was being shaken by the gentleman and then she was embraced -yes embraced - by the two young ladies. Well, hugged, enthusiastically, by the younger one. The eldest girl smiled and gave her a very gentle hug and murmured "I hope you will not find having two sisters overwhelming."

Jane laughed. A brittle laugh to be sure. *What do I do now?*

The next thing Jane knew, Sir Richard had bundled her into her cloak, it had finally dried, and her sad mostly ruined bonnet and her boots, which were dry and toasty warm for being near the fireplace. A guard was placed in front of the fire. Sir Richard then donned his coat and hat, which were no doubt rather damp since he spent so much time out tending to the cattle and bringing in firewood. Then they were off in a large sleigh pulled by two handsome, bay, draft horses.

Warm bricks on the floor of the sleigh warmed their feet and woolen rugs, tightly woven in colorful patterns, kept them all snug and warm. The snow had stopped, and the sun was out, and the icy limbs of the trees and shrubs sparkled like diamonds on the entire ride to the church.

The service was much like any other Sunday service, as Jane had been to many of them, although only at this one people looked at her with much curiosity. Sir Richard's ring was still on her finger, over her ruined gloves which were smudged with dirt. It was much too large, of course, but for those who saw it, and everyone was looking at her finger, she knew, it gave out the message with no one saying a word to her or asking a question. She, for the first time in over a year, felt safe and protected. And, unsure.

For his part, Sir Richard is smiling as if this is the happiest day of his life. As if he really wants to marry me. I do not know how to feel. I do not know what to say. I feel like such a fraud.

Now the service was over, and Jane was feeling overwhelmed as people were shaking his hand, shaking her hand, kissing her cheek, saying "Who would have thought?" and congratulating both of them. And then they were back in the sleigh and on their way back to where? The cottage?

"Well, that was fun" Sir Richard said to her, an easy smile on his face, his voice gentle. "You will like the dinner our cook has waiting for us. Goose is her specialty, although many say her duck and pheasant are also good. Is there one you prefer, my dear?"

"I have never had pheasant," Jane said, wondering if she should also confess that she had never had goose or duck, either. They had had chickens and pigeons for their fare had been simple. They had had enough to live on but there were few extras when her parents had been alive and none after they had died.

"Does-did-your father have a large library?" he asked her, his voice gentle, as his mother and the squire were caught up in discussing those who had gone to the church service, none of whom Jane knew, of course.

"Yes, very extensive, mainly about antiquities," she said, and added "They spoke of selling the books in London."

"I will purchase them, never you worry about that, my dear, and have them transported to the Hall. I have many empty shelves in my library and if we run out of room, we will just annex an adjoining room and expand the collection."

Then he added, "As soon as we reach the Hall, Miss Smith, I will send men out to rescue our cattle and bring them to the barn for warm mash and a brisk rubdown. No doubt they are feeling rather cold and neglected. The cart is thoroughly destroyed. I will have it replaced."

Chapter 10

Richard was rejoicing in his good luck. He had found the perfect wife for him. She shared his interests and with her help he could expand his collection to include more than just coins, though coins would always be his primary interest.

He noted that she is comely. Not classically beautiful, perhaps, she nevertheless is pleasing to look at with a smile that can light up a room, those few times she really smiled today. Maybe they would suit.

Or, she could be an assistant to him. She might not wish to marry. He would have to think upon it and come to a decision soon. He hated to put off important decisions.

His mother and the squire, who were no doubt curious to know more about Miss Smith, kept up a running commentary on mundane things such as the unusually snowy month and this morning's sermon.

And then the sleigh arrived at the hall.

"Here we are, my dear, Weatherby Hall."

The large grey stone building rose up four stories and was square in shape in the center with two wings on either side. The steps leading up to the front door were well weathered and partially worn from all of the feet that had traversed them for hundreds of years. The building was quite old, centuries in fact, although the inside had been modernized.

"I know it shows its age in wear on the outside, my dear, but the inside is quite cheerful and modern, you will see" Sir Richard said and after following Mr. Howard out of the sleigh, he turned and offering her his hand, smiled into her eyes and whispered, "it will be all right, trust me."

As Mr. Howard assisted Sir Richard's mother out of the sleigh and the young ladies were assisted out by a footman, Sir Richard guided Jane up the stairs and explained the layout of Weatherby Hall to her.

Sir Richard presented her to the butler as his future bride and said "Ah, Sims, please ask Mrs. Anders to come here. I wish to make known to her my future bride."

"Very good, Sir Richard, Miss" the tall rather stately man said, and gave her a second look before he walked towards the furthest end of the main hallway.

"Mrs. Anders is our housekeeper. You will find her to be most pleasant," he said, her arm tucked through his.

Chapter 11

Her arm through his, Jane felt more at ease and not as frightened. *Perhaps everything will be all right. Somehow.*

I wonder if he can feel me shivering with fear and yes, with excitement, too. I will worry tomorrow. It is just so much at once.

Several moments later, a cheerful, tall, rather thin woman, dressed in a black dress emerged from the back of the hallway and walked towards them, a large smile on her face. "Welcome to Weatherby Hall, Miss," she said and turning to Sir Richard said "You rascal, you can not give a body any warning, can you? Do not worry I will have a splendid guest room prepared in a thrice and a lovely dinner for the holiday and to welcome your bride to be."

"Miss Smith will need a hot bath and a maid, Mrs. Anders," Sir Richard said to the woman who looked directly at Jane.

"I have just the maid for you, Miss, and there will be a nice hot bath for you directly."

A few footmen walked by on errands and looking over with curiosity continued on with whatever errand they were on.

Sir Richard's sisters were talking excitedly with their mother and Mr. Howard as they ascended the staircase.

"Uh, Mother, and oh, Holly, could you both spare me a moment of your time right now?" Sir Richard asked his mother before she had gone more than a few steps up.

"Of course, dear," his mother said. She, the squire and Holly returned to stand with Sir Richard and Jane in the hallway.

Jane, not knowing what to do, tried to look at ease, but it was difficult. No luggage, no clothing, no place to go and no coin to purchase any of that. *Nothing. I have nothing. I do not even own the clothing I am wearing except my boots, gloves, cloak, and bonnet. And I have nowhere to go.*

Sir Richard, however, had things well in hand.

"Mother, Holly, Jane is in dire straits at this time. While on her way to visit us so we could stage a grand surprise of our engagement, her luggage fell off of her conveyance and landed in the brook and was ruined. Could you not lend her some clothing until hers can be replaced?"

"Of course. Oh, you poor dear," his mother said, turning to Jane and hugging her, "How awful to lose your own clothing. You and Holly are of a size. I am sure Holly has some things to fit you."

"Please be discrete," Sir Richard said, at which point both women started laughing. He looked puzzled.

"Son, both of the girls know what the other owns, so we will just explain, and no one will think a thing of it." Turning, she put Jane's arm through hers and urged her to go with her and Holly up the stairs, leaving the men behind.

"Mrs. Anders has put you in the lilac room. I am sure you will find it perfectly wonderful. The room is painted in cream, but the view is of lilacs in the spring, hence the name" his mother said as they halted in front of a door.

Jane followed his mother into a beautiful room with a southern view that would bring in sunshine during the day through one window and a view of the dawn, no doubt, through the one on the adjoining wall.

"This is lovely" Jane murmured, while looking around the room. There was a wardrobe off of the bedroom and a bathing room, too. Holly took her to look about the rooms for they were more luxurious than anything Jane had ever seen in her life. The bedroom itself had a dressing table and comfortable armchair, the kind one likes to sit in and dream of happy places, a fireplace with a cheery wood fire in it and a small desk.

"Come to my room, Jane. I may call you that, might I?" Holly asked and not waiting for an answer grabbed Jane's arm and literally pulled her out of the room and up the hallway. "I have a number of dresses I never wear, and we are of a size."

Richard's mother smothered a laugh. *Jane seems to be the perfect wife for Richard*, she thought. Sweet, soft spoken and not easily offended by two lively girls who should be acting more like ladies than girls. *No doubt there is a good story behind this,* she thought, for she knew that the story that her son had dredged up at what was most likely the last minute in desperation, was pure fiddle-faddle.

Chapter 12

At dinner, Jane was bewildered as course followed course. There was goose to begin with, and then several removes, ending with fruit. *Mama and papa would have been happy with just the goose and a few more dishes*, she found herself thinking. *I had not realized how simple a life we were living.* By watching what utensils everyone else was using for each dish, Jane was able to not make a faux pas.

Richard watched Jane eating her food. *She is hungry but is careful to follow suit with each course. A clever woman.* His admiration for her rose even higher.

Chapter 13

After the women had retired to the parlour and the two men, for Mr. Howard had remained for dinner, were seated at the table sipping brandy, Sir Richard asked for a favor.

"I am glad you stayed here this evening, for I have a vexing problem to solve."

Richard did not know if his widowed mother would ever remarry but she had chosen well in her choice of a male friend. Mr. Howard was a widower and he and his wife and Richard's parents had been fast friends. Now the two of them were left behind by the deaths of their respective spouses and went to balls and other entertainments together. Might they one day marry? Maybe, but he wondered if maybe his mother wanted to get the girls married and into homes of their own first. She had been after him to marry since the mourning period for his father had ended.

Briefly he filled Mr. Howard in on how he had found Jane and what her circumstances entailed, including a decision he had just made concerning Jane and her circumstances.

The two men sat in silence for a few moments. A fire crackled in the grate.

Mr. Howard spoke first. "Of course, you did the right thing, Sir Richard, in announcing your engagement immediately.

Otherwise, she would have been quite ruined. And she can call off the engagement without any harm whereas you can not and that might be a problem."

"How so?"

"If you do not wish to marry the girl, and I believe you do not."

"Quite so." Though a part of him was not so certain he wanted to let her go.

Mayhap he had accidentally found his bride? Or not. *Mayhap I need a bride with more, well, just more, but I can not think of what else I need in a wife. I will know when I find her.* He remembered Jane nestled against his body in the night and she had felt just right. Like she belonged here. With him. It had taken all his resolve to not seduce her. He had not slept well most of that night.

She might not want me for a husband. She might have other dreams.

Mr. Howard again broke the silence.

"What will you do if she does not call off the engagement? She has not yet, and she had many opportunities today."

"She will" Richard said confidently. *Will she be happy buried in the country? I like a quiet life.*

Mr. Howard looked doubtful but kept his consul. The men joined the ladies.

Richard was pleased to see that Miss Smith, who had come to dinner dressed in a becoming gown that he recognized as belonging to one of his sisters, was chatting with his mother. Everyone seems quite at ease. *All is well in my world*, he thought, *what can go wrong?*

Chapter 14

Jane loved her room. Her maid Sally, the first maid she had ever had, was cheerful and asked no questions. Sally acted as if not having luggage and wearing borrowed clothing was normal.

The view was wonderful, and the bed was so comfortable. She should have slept well. *After all, I have a nice bed, a splendid room and I am engaged to Sir Richard. A very nice man who shares my passion for artifacts. It is too good to be true.*

But Jane missed something. The feel of a warm, naked man next to her. *How lowering to not be able to sleep because he is not here. Is that the way he usually sleeps? Naked? Or does he wear a nightshirt? Why do I care? He can not really want to marry me. Can he?*

Finally, Jane fell asleep and dreamt. Not happy dreams. No, in her dreams men were chasing her and chanting "hang her. Hang her." She awoke in the morning feeling like she had not slept at all. *I need to leave here. I can not marry Sir Richard. I am wanted as a horse thief. They will hang me. He and his family have been so kind to me. I can not bring disgrace on them. I have to leave. Mayhap I have a few more days to stay while I decide what to do. I do not have references. Whatever will happen to me?*

SIR RICHARD MEETS HIS MATCH

Chapter 15

The next day dawned bright and cold.

The knocker dropped on the door and Sims let in two men. "Is Sir Richard at home?" one of them asked?

When asked who was calling the men announced that they were pursuing a horse thief. A young woman who had stolen a pony and cart.

Sims nodded and said he would see if Sir Richard was at home, and he went in search of him.

Upstairs in the hallway, on her way to the parlour for tea, Jane stood with her hands to her mouth. Her nightmare was upon her only it is real life. *They are here to take me away. I have to leave now!*

Seeing Sims approaching, Jane asked if Sir. Richard was in his office.

Sims passed her in the hallway, "I would suggest you might like to await Sir Richard in the library, Miss. Sir Richard has visitors," he said.

"Thank you, Sims, I think I will retire to my room" Jane said.

"Very good, Miss," he said and continued along the hallway to Sir Richard's office, where he found Sir Richard looking over the estate books.

"Ah, yes, I was expecting something like this, Sims," Sir Richard said. "This saves me the trouble of finding them." He sounded somewhat cheerful.

Jane continued to her own room, her borrowed room, she thought wryly. She waited a few minutes and then stole out into the hall and then to Sir Richard's office and paused outside the door. *Should I go in and see what they have to say?*

Through the door she heard one of the men say, "It's a hanging offense, Sir Richard." Her heart began to pound in her ears.

She fled.

Changing her borrowed shoes for her own boots, she put on her heavy wool cloak and bonnet and gloves and quietly stole down the back servant's stairs.

She ran through the snow to the barn. There she said that Sir

Richard wanted Dusty hitched to a small cart so she could make a trip into the village.

The head groomsman, Bill, wanted to send a groom with her. She politely, but firmly, declined any escort.

"You do not know the way to the village, Miss," he said, concerned that she was setting out on her own alone, "and I could hitch up a team to a sleigh and one of the groomsmen will take you there and back again."

"Oh, I know the way, I remember the way from the church" she said and thanked him for assisting her into the cart. "I do not need a sleigh. We will be fine. It is only a short way."

She left the stable and waved to the men as they went back inside. That is when the tears started. She was afraid and urged Dusty to walk faster. The going was difficult because of the snow and drifting but Dusty trudged through each little mound and kept on toward the main road.

Not only was she a horse thief, but she was also stealing one of Sir Richard's carts. Her life was one big nightmare. If only she could think of a good plan. Her instinct was to flee.

"When I get to the main road which way should I go? Will they think I am returning to my village, or will they think I am going to London?" she asked Dusty. Dusty just twitched his ears as she pondered that as they continued along the long drive.

Chapter 16

"Sir Richard will not like this," the head groomsman thought, and turning to a stable lad, bade him to saddle up a Roman for Sir Richard. "No," he said under his breath, "Sir Richard will not like this at all." He then sent a stable lad up to inform Sir Richard that the young lady had left in the pony cart.

In his office, Sir Richard was shaking hands with the two men after concluding their business. It has been as he had supposed with a new wrinkle. Mr. Howard, who had come for tea, was his witness. They were all smiling as the men were shown out of the room and the down to the front door by Sims.

"Let us have some tea with the ladies," Sir Richard said to Mr. Howard, "then I think I will have a word alone with Miss Smith.

"Sir Richard was most accommodating," one of the men said to the other, as they mounted their horses and headed back out on the drive that led to the main road.

Chapter 17

Jane reached the end of the drive and had to decide which way to go. "Sir Richard will tell them we are going to London" she said aloud to Dusty, for she often spoke to him. In response Dusty twitched his ears.

"We will go in the opposite direction then" she said and turned Dusty back along the road that led back to her own little village. "There is a crossroads past our own village leading towards larger towns, though none as large as London. She had thought she could hide in London. Mayhap I can find a position in a coaching inn as a maid. I am sure I will not need references for that kind of position."

Jiggling the reins, she looked behind her as Dusty dutifully trotted along the lane, which was not as difficult to traverse due to sleighs which had packed down some of the snow.

"Hurry, Dusty" Jane pleaded with her pony. There was no way that they could pass through their old village and reach the next large town before darkness unless they hurried.

What if it is the men looking for me?

She said out loud "we have to hide, Dusty" and then realized that there was nowhere to hide. If they left the trail, they would leave tracks in the snow. And they also could not leave the lane because the wheels would get bogged down in the snow drifts. She really needed a sleigh.

"What are we going to do, Dusty?" she asked, as she started to shake with fear.

She knew she would hang if it were those two men behind her. She was afraid to look back.

Reaching the turn off for the little hut, Jane pulled on the reins. "There are horses on the lane behind us Dusty, but the tracks to the hut are almost obliterated by the snow. The cart will get stuck if we try to go back there."

She sat on the seat of the cart not knowing what to do. Dusty just shook his head and calmly waited for Jane to make a decision.

The horses were coming along and would catch up to them soon. Whatever could she do?

There was nowhere to hide. If she left Dusty, they could follow her footprints in the snow.

"We have to try, Dusty, maybe they will think it is someone else." And she urged Dusty onto the little track to the hut.

Chapter 18

When the men reached the end of the lane, they pulled up their horses for a moment and one of them speculated that they might be better off staying at an inn.

"I do not think there is an inn in such a small village." the other man said. "We can be back before full dark if we hurry, I am sure.

The day was still early enough that it was safe to canter homeward and they turned their horses in that direction in the hopes of reaching their home village before nightfall.

Meanwhile a concerned Sir Richard arrived at the stables. "Where did she go?" Richard asked, as he mounted his horse. Fortunately, his groomsman had had Roman saddled and ready to go when Richard arrived at the stable.

"To the village" the head groomsman said, as Richard nudged the horse forward.

Urging Roman into a gallop down the lane, he headed toward the village.

They had not gone too far when the men came upon Miss Smith and her pony. The cart had become hopelessly mired in a deep bank of snow.

They dismounted and approaching the cart cheerfully called out to her.

Chapter 19

Richard reached the village. He knew that the Jenkin sisters, who lived in the cottage just past the church, saw everything that went on in view of their front window and everyone who rode by.

Dismounting, he rapped on the door. There was nothing for it, he had to drink a cup of scalding tea, his throat would be sore for a few days, no doubt, and eat a scone that was partly made of rock, he would swear, before he could get the ladies to give him an accounting of all who passed by their windows.

No, no young lady in a pony cart had come by way of the lane. Why did he want to know?

Why indeed. "She is, uh, a friend of my sisters and we were, uh, expecting her. I, uh, must conclude that she, umm, stayed home due to the inclement weather," he finished lamely. Telling lies was not a specialty of his.

"You said she was coming into the village from your estate."

"Oh, did I? I, uh, meant she might have gone past our lane and mistakenly, um, come to the village. No doubt she found the snow too deep and stayed at home," he said and rose to take his leave.

They watched from their front window as Sir Richard mounted his horse and headed back the way he had come.

"Why do you think he was lying to us, Amelia?"

"I do not know, Hattie. It will be most interesting to learn more about this girl with the pony cart. We will have to have our niece who works at Sir Richard's estate to tea soon."

"Yes, indeed, there is something going on there."

"I wonder what it is."

Sir Richard urged his horse back towards the estate at as fast a clip as was safe. The wind was slicing through his clothing, and he found himself shivering. Ordinarily he did not mind the cold. "It will be a cold night, Roman," he said to his horse. "I hope I find her before nightfall."

When he reached the lane to his estate, he urged Roman on by. He could clearly see that several horses and the tracks of a small wagon had gone that way. He should have looked closely when he initially rode to the village. He cursed under his breath. He had been too sure of her direction and in too much of a hurry to think of looking for the tracks.

Chapter 20

The two men rode towards her.

Jane knew what would happen next. Dusty would be taken to his new owner, and she would be brought before the magistrate. She would no doubt hang or be transported. She hung her head.

The tears fell freely down her face and her hands trembled on the reins -the now useless reins.

After the men had managed to free the cart from a drift, Jane found herself once more in the cart on the main road.

"I know you said you have a friend down that lane, Miss Smith, but there is no way that little pony can pull you and the cart down that track, Best if you go back to the Hall, Miss Smith."

The men were being kind to her. Jane had expected them to rail at her and to call her a thief at any moment. *At least no one from the estate will witness me being taken away to the magistrate. No one will know my shame of being labeled a thief.*

Just when she thought the worst had happened, the worse did happen as Sir Richard rode up to them, mounted his magnificent gelding, as the two men's horses were standing next to the pony cart.

Not only am I to be taken before a magistrate, will I be humiliated in front of Sir Richard. It was too much to be borne. Jane burst into tears again. *I am going to hang now that I have been caught.*

SIR RICHARD MEETS HIS MATCH

Chapter 21

Within moments, Richard was down off of his horse and climbing up onto the seat of the cart. He put his arms around her and murmured "You poor dear. You must be exhausted."

She felt, well, safe. She knew she was going to be arrested but she still, in his arms, felt safe. And, cared for. How odd.

Richard saw the tracks in the snow. She had tried to reach the hut. He shook his head. Poor Jane.

"You can run as far and as fast as you wish, but you can not escape me unless you want to," he said to her, as she leaned against him.

He was warm and she was so cold. Her teeth were now chattering, and her tears had, once again, crystallized on her cheeks.

Pulling some pound notes from inside his coat he handed them to the two men and thanked them for their help in rescuing Miss Smith.

"It is a pleasure, Sir Richard, doing business with you," one of the men said.

"Good luck Miss Smith," the other man said.

And then the two men sent their horses into a canter and left them alone.

"We had better be getting back to the Hall," Richard said as he gently wiped her face with his gloved fingertips and released her.

He unhitched Dusty and he took the long reins in his hands. Mounting Roman, he rode closer to her and reaching down said "Just relax while I pull you up in front of me. You will be quite safe."

Jane could not believe what was happening. The men left her. They were civil to her and they left her with Sir Richard. And now Sir Richard was going to pull her up in front of him on his horse. *How scandalous*, she thought, although she was too cold, too tired, too dispirited to care. *Perhaps Sir Richard is the local magistrate, and I am going to be held at the Hall until my trial.*

Sir Richard hoisted her up and she found herself sitting sideways in front of him. She was not afraid of falling as he had one arm firmly around her.

"Now, Miss Smith, I want you to just relax. You are as stiff as the poker in front of my fireplace. I will not let you fall. I promise you will be safe."

She almost laughed. She was not afraid of falling, even though they were very high on that horse, she was afraid of hanging. *Would it hurt? Much?*

Or maybe Sir Richard is going to take her to the magistrate tomorrow. Oh, how lowering that this man, this wonderful, kind, loving man, is now to be her jailor, for he had said he was taking her to the Hall.

He walked Roman back to the drive that led to the stables, leading Dusty by the long reins.

"I will send someone for the cart tomorrow. No one will take it. If it is stolen, I can replace it. Do not fret."

He could feel her shivering in his arms. Her teeth were chattering. He could not see her face because her bonnet rim was too large, and her face was turned away from him.

Chapter 22

When they reached the stables, Richard rode up to the mounting block and asked Bill, the head groomsman, to help Miss Smith down off of Roman. The groomsman then took Dusty and Roman to the barn.

Richard, taking hold of Jane by the arm, said, "I think a spot of tea will be in order and some of Cook's scrumptious cakes and then a hot bath followed by a nap and then supper and a long night's sleep are in order for you. We can talk about this tomorrow. And, Miss Smith, no one is going to hurt you. You have my word." And, smiling cheerfully, he gave her arm a squeeze.

Instead of a flurry of snow, Jane found herself engulfed in wool and muslin, perfume and arms as Sir Richard's sisters hugged her and fussed over her as if she was the prodigal sister and had returned after being away for years instead of a mere few hours.

"Now, girls, let Miss Smith catch her breath" Jane heard Sir Richard's mother say and extricating Jane from the girls arms she led Jane to the parlour where a roaring fire warmed the room more than usual, the girls trailing behind them.

"I thought you might be cold, and I had the fire built up and, oh, here is the tea tray. Come sit down by the fire and sip hot tea" Sir Richard's mother said, scarcely stopping for breath.

Suiting words to action, his mother poured her tea, fixed it just the way she liked it and brought it to her while the girls tried to interest her in some small cakes.

"I, uh, I do not think..."

"Girls, leave Jane alone. She has had an ordeal and let her breathe."

The girls were curious. Jane noted that they looked at each other and then at her but true to their mother's command to not fuss over her, they now sat demurely and sipped their tea. "Such a nice family. I wish I could be part of it."

"We do too," Lily said, smiling. Her eyes twinkling.

"Oh, dear," Jane exclaimed, "did I just say that out loud? Whatever must you think of me?"

"We like you," Holly added. "We hope that Richard, who can be addlepated at times, marries you."

After a moment of thought, Lily then said with enthusiasm, "Oh, can you get married here on the estate? We could decorate the chapel and have a..."

"Girls, please. No one is talking about getting married. Now say your apologies."

The girls did, prettily, but they were smiling and clearly thinking of a wedding, one between her and Sir Richard.

How wonderful that would be. How unlikely. How impossible, Jane was thinking at that moment,

Jane was also thinking of the hangman's noose that literally hung over her head. Or maybe transportation to a faraway land where she did not know anyone. Either way she knew she was going to die and nearly teared up again.

As soon as Jane finished her tea, Sir Richard's mother ordered hot water and then she was in the bath and warming up. The bed looked so inviting and soon she was tucked into bed wearing a fine linen nightshift that must belong to one of the girls, as Jane had never seen it before.

"Now get some rest," Sally said, "and ring when you are hungry, and I will have a supper tray brought up to you. You have had quite an ordeal, or so I have been told."

As Jane snuggled down under the covers, following a simple but hearty supper, she was grateful to his mother for she had arranged for the bed to be warmed for her and she then fell asleep.

Chapter 23

Sir Richard's mother was, at that point, sitting in Sir Richard's office. "To come to the point, Richard, why did Miss Smith run away from you?"

"A misunderstanding, perhaps. I really do not know." he said.

"You must tell me everything because something has frightened that poor girl and I think you know what it is."

"I do."

"Then tell me."

"That is her personal business, Mother."

"It is now my business so you will tell me. Her running away has made it so."

"Has it now," he said, not really asking. Of course, his mother was correct.

"And your sisters are presently planning a wedding for the two of you, so I need some answers. I need them now."

At that, Richard burst into laughter. "Chose my bride for me, did they?"

He continued, "There was a misunderstanding, of sorts, Mother. Miss Smith was turned out of her home by her cousin. I suspect her cousin did not know who the occupant was. I have met him in the past and he seems to be a decent sort. The men who came here were to collect her and the pony and cart.

"I have dealt with them, and they will bother her no more.

And I have sent a missive to her cousin explaining the situation. I am sure we will hear from him in short order."

His mother, satisfied with his answer, smiled.

Chapter 24

Upstairs Jane was dreaming. She was in a chapel and Sir Richard was standing in front of the altar to make her his bride and the vicar turned and was holding instead of a bible, a hangman's noose. She screamed.

There was a scratching at the door and Holly looked in when Jane called out "enter."

"I heard you scream" Holly said. "Is there anything I can do to help? It must be scary to be all alone in the world."

Sitting up in bed, Jane said, "I do not feel all alone when I am here with all of you here. I had a bad dream. I am sorry if I woke you up."

"I was awake looking out my window at the moonlit snow outside the hall" Holly said to her. "It is so pretty. It looks like a magical place. It is as if the buildings and trees had cake frosting on them."

"Or cream?" Jane asked, smiling. "I am so happy you came to my room. I now feel much better. Thank you."

"Good night," Holly said, and quietly left the room.

Feeling much better, Jane lay down and fell asleep.

Chapter 25

When Jane next awoke, it was a bright sunny day. The world appeared to be decorated in sparkling diamonds. It had snowed a little during the night and it was in fluffy mounds on the outside window ledge. Jane stood at the window idly tracing the intricate patterns of frost on the window, lost in thought, and not enjoying the beauty of the scene before her. *Whatever is going to happen to me?*

There was a scratching on the door and Sally walked in with a tray containing a cup of hot chocolate, along with the greeting, "The family is starting to gather for breakfast, Miss."

Soon Jane was dressed in a warm woolen day dress the color of a deep blue sky. She descended the stairs, dreading the ordeal of learning what her fate would be. *Residing in an unheated cell in the nearest town or maybe here as the "guest" of Sir Richard until her day to be sentenced?*

And in the back of Jane's mind was the thought that it was almost Christmas and she had no gifts for Sir Richard, his mother or his delightful sisters. *If only I could be part of this wonderful, warm, loving, family. Sir Richard has announced to all that I am his betrothed, but I know that was only to protect my reputation. Such a good man. It is time I set him free. I should have done that long before, then, he would not have felt the need to go after me. Mayhap he feels he needs to defend me? Could that be? No, I must be held here for the magistrate. Sir Richard would not have been able to bribe those men. He is too honorable, is he not?*

As Jane walked into the room she was greeted with smiles and was soon sitting again to the right of Sir Richard at the table and eating a hearty breakfast and drinking tea.

"I hope you do not mind, Miss Smith," Sir Richard said, "We have never gotten into the habit of drinking coffee for breakfast."

"We, that is, I, always drink tea. I do not think I have ever had coffee before I met you..."

Mr. Howard, who was, it seemed, a frequent visitor, was watching her, she realized, and when she looked into his face he smiled and winked at her.

That wink tells me he knows more than I want him to know.

Her parents never had a large yule log, like some homes did, but they did keep a twig from the previous year's log on the eve of Christmas to light the new small yule log each year.

The smell of baking filled the house. The cook was in her element come Christmas every year, Holly told her, a smile of anticipation of the celebration to come on her face.

Jane joined in the laughter as Sir Richard found himself besieged by his sisters to join them in gathering greenery, and soon they all were off on sleds into the woods where they spent nearly two hours gathering greens to bring home.

There was a lot of laughing and joking. The girls included Jane in their search for greens. The two men, along with some servants, were able to get greenery from the higher branches. Even Sir Richard's mother got in the spirit of gathering the fragrant greens as well.

A yule log was procured by servants who also joined in the fun and then it was back to the Hall.

Then the decorating began in earnest after a hearty tea. The girls were giggling as Sir Richard's mother supervised the hanging of the greenery, although the girls seemed to have the upper hand at times. It was not long before there were greens everywhere, including one large garland wrapped around the banister of the stairs on one side.

"Oh, look, there is something caught in the floorboard, Lily"

said as Sir Richard was passing by Jane in the front hall. He stopped to look. "I do not see anything."

"Jane, you see it, do you not?" the girl asked, all innocence.

Jane peered down at the floor and then became aware of some giggling followed by "Look up."

Mistletoe hung in a ball above their heads. Sir Richard laughed. Jane blushed.

"Kiss her" one of the girls said followed by a "yes. kiss her by the other.

Jane and Sir Richard looked at each other, speechless.

"Girls, girls, leave them alone" his mother said, a smile in her voice.

Richard took Jane's trembling hands in his. "Well?" he said, smiling.

"I, that is we, uh, do not have a choice. Do we?" she asked, her voice a little unsteady. *I can not think of anything I would rather do than kiss him, alone,* Jane thought as she nodded, and then looked down, embarrassed.

Then she raised her chin a bit, feeling suddenly very shy.

My first kiss and I have to share it with his family.

And she blushed.

She is shy. Tilting her chin up with his fingers Richard looked deep into her eyes. They darkened. *She is passionate,* he thought, noting a hitch in her breath as he put his lips to hers for a small moment of bliss.

As kisses went, it was very chaste. With his mother and sisters looking on, there was no choice in the matter. There was applause and then everyone went on their way, Jane, also, though she stopped and looked back at him for a moment. He could not read the look in her eyes. *Did she enjoy it? Regret it? I wonder.*

"As soon as her cousin arrives, I will talk with her," he told his mother when she questioned him on when he was planning on talking with Miss Smith. "I need to know all of the particulars."

He noted a small smile on his mother's face. He knew that smile. It meant that she had made up her mind about something but would not share it until she was ready. She had always been that way.

He wondered if Mr. Howard would ever come up to scratch. *Or is he waiting for the girls to be married off?*

Chapter 26

Jane went to her room for a quiet nap. She needed to decide what she could do in London without references if she were let go. She had no friends there. *Whatever will I do? He does not really wish to marry me; he just did not want to embarrass me in front of his mother and sisters and Mr. Howard. Sir Richard is a good man. Too good for someone like me. And I will bring disgrace to him if I am hung for horse stealing.*

She should not have left with Dusty. *What a fool I was. I will lose him and mayhap my life too. Mayhap the vicar could have found me a living as a companion somewhere. Why did I do that?*

She lay on the top of the bedding and cried and fell into an uneasy sleep.

Jane awoke a little before tea would be served. *I will leave tomorrow. I do not know where I will go but I will leave a note breaking our engagement and leave. I can not tell him myself. I know he will try to convince me to stay. Heaven knows I want to stay. Here. With him.*

Chapter 27

The Christmas morning service had always been one of her favorites, but that morning, all she could think about was how she did not want to die. She was frightened about hanging. *It will hurt,* she was thinking. *I am going to die. I do not want to die. I want to live.*

She looked up and saw that Sir Richard was watching her. He smiled. She smiled back. On her hand, over her glove, his ring was there on her finger. He had insisted. People were watching them, and she saw some nudging each other with smiles on their faces. *They think we are truly engaged. They expect to see us wed. Oh, poor Sir Richard, when I have to jilt him. I should have done that yesterday.*

He leaned down and whispered, "We will talk in my office after nuncheon."

Jane nodded her head in the affirmative. *I do not really want to know my fate but not knowing is even worse. Maybe transportation. Or maybe it is the hulks for me. Or the tower?*

After the service, once again, Sir Richard whisked her away before anyone could say too much to them. His mother and Mr. Howard also came over to the sleigh in a brisk manner.

"People are talking," she said to Sir Richard. "We will have to let them know something soon."

Jane did not know what to say. So, she said nothing.

"Soon enough, Mother," he said. "I do not dance attendance on the village."

"I am not sure your sisters have been too indiscreet and..."

"Mother, do not fret. All will be well. I am not concerned."

"I only" his mother said and then fell silent after a stern look from Sir Richard, and no one spoke the remainder of the way.

It was a beautiful day where the sun shone brightly, and the snow lay deep beside the road. The horses pulled the sleighs effortlessly along the lane.

Ordinarily, Jane would have loved the sleigh ride but she was too afraid of what was going to happen after Sir Richard took her to the magistrate's office. Wherever it was.

After nuncheon, true to his word, Sir Richard invited her to his office. For the sake of propriety, though it was rather late for that, he supposed, he invited his mother to join them.

"What is your mother's maiden name?" he asked Jane.

"Why?"

"Just humor me for a moment. What was her surname?"

"Miller. Her name was Miller."

"Do you know a William Miller?"

"No."

"Are you sure?"

"No, Yes, I mean I do not know, oh wait, I think there is a cousin William somewhere."

"My dear. There was a terrible misunderstanding on someone's part."

"There was?"

He started by asking her questions. This puzzled her but she answered readily. Yes, her parents died just over a year ago in a carriage accident. No, she did not see a copy of her father's will. She did not know that there had even been a will. And, no, she did not send information to her cousin William because she did not know who to contact about the cottage.

Then he asked how she had been living, there, alone in the cottage with no income. She smiled. She had raised a few chickens and traded eggs for milk and flour. She traded mending in exchange for firewood and was very careful with everything. She had some coins her parents had put by in case of emergencies. She was, in fact, reaching the end of the coins when the men had arrived and said she was to leave there and to leave everything. "They did not believe me when I said that I owned Dusty and the cart and ordered me to leave everything and to go." She dabbed at her eyes as tears started to fall.

"It was all most likely a silly mistake" Sir Richard said, gently, handing her a handkerchief. "No doubt your cousin only realized that he owned your cottage recently and was told that it was empty. He did not know he had family living there, I would guess. I have sent a missive to him to find out how to proceed. He may offer you a roof over your head and a place in his family, seeing how you are alone in the world and that he appears to be your only known kin. At this time."

"At this time?" Jane asked, relieved to know that there was at least one family member left in the world.

"I am making inquiries on your behalf, I hope you do not mind, to see if your father also has family in England. You might still have other family members who will take you in.

SIR RICHARD MEETS HIS MATCH

"I did not know any family members on either side of the family. But, but, that is, they still think I stole Dusty and the cart. That is a... a...hanging offense."

"Oh, my poor dear," Sir Richard's mother said, up until this moment being quiet, "Nothing is going to happen to you. Nothing like that. Tell her, Richard."

"Is this true?" Jane asked, as she looked from his mother to Sir Richard.

"Yes, it is true," he said. "I stretched the truth a tad. I said that I had purchased the pony and cart from your father and was awaiting delivery before paying for it. That you were just doing that, delivering them to me. That the money was going to the estate owner. They went away happy."

"Oh. I. That is..." Jane stopped talking, closed her eyes, thought through what he had said, opened her eyes and asked, "Does that mean that I am not a horse thief anymore?"

"I think your mother's cousin inherited your cottage along with several other small properties and he never made an effort, himself, to inspect all of the properties he inherited. On the advice of a solicitor, I suppose, he decided to sell off or rent the minor properties..."

"Those men? They wanted to take Dusty back and... and...and..." Jane could not help it she burst into tears.

His mother came over to her and sat next to her on the small settee and put her arms around her, holding her close.

Jane felt safe, for a moment. Composing herself, she then asked, "What did the men want, then?"

"Yes, they were here to retrieve Dusty, the cart, and you" he said. He looked down at a paper on his desk. Then he looked up.

"I have a man checking to see if this William Miller is, indeed, related to you. I have had some inquiries made and am awaiting the answers. In the meantime, I did something I do not like to do. I told a slight, uh, mistruth. "

"You did? Because of me?"

"Yes," he said, but he did not look too unhappy.

"That...that means that I, uh, that I..."

"Yes, that you are free, my dear. The pony, Dusty, and the cart are now legally yours. I had the papers drawn up." He sat back, looking very pleased with himself.

Jane threw her arms around his mother's neck and sobbed tears of joy. His mother threw him a look. "You could have told her sooner, dearest" she said.

"I, well, I did not think that one more day or two would make any difference."

Sir Richard stood and came over and took both her hands in his. "I am sorry I did not tell you yesterday that I was having inquiries made. I did not want to get your hopes up as I only had the papers signed yesterday afternoon and you were so tired and... and...and...I am sorry my dear. Happy Christmas."

"Happy Christmas, Sir Richard" she said and looked up into his eyes. She remembered the kiss then and blushed. She wondered if there was a way to steer him under the mistletoe again. "Thank you. Thank you for giving me back my life. For saving my life."

Chapter 28

He looked down at her and wished there was a way he could get her under some mistletoe. He wanted to kiss her again. Hells, bells, he wanted to do more than kiss her.

Someone dropped the knocker on the door. They could hear it faintly from the office.

Then they heard the murmur of voices getting closer. A footman entered the room and spoke quietly to Sir Richard.

"A family member of Miss Jane's has just arrived to clear up the matter of her cottage," Richard told Jane and his mother. "I have suggested he await us in the parlour and have ordered the tea trolley."

They adjourned to the parlour and standing in front of the fire, awaiting them, was a young man with sandy colored hair and eyes the same color as Jane's.

"Sir Richard, I am William Miller and I have arrived to correct a great wrong I have done, unintentionally, to my second cousin, Miss Jane Smith," the man said without preamble.

"Very good, let us be seated and we can talk while we indulge in a cup of tea and my cook's famous tarts," Richard said as they all seated themselves, the gentlemen after the ladies, of course.

"I am so sorry, Miss Smith, I did not know the cottage was being used, much less by a member of my family, I do beg your pardon and hope you will forgive me."

"Of course, Mr. Miller," Jane said, "I have been busy just getting through the year and mourning my parents. I should have tried to find out who inherited. I, I did not think on it. I thought my father owned the cottage."

"The cottage was given to your parents during their lifetime. I did not know you existed. I thought the cottage was empty or taken over by strangers. I do beg your pardon."

"Then I can return to the cottage?" Jane asked, breaking into a radiant smile.

"Uh, no, that is, I promised the cottage to my head gardener and his wife, as he is retiring, and they have family living in the village. I will, of course, return your belongings to you. Just tell me where to send them."

"Oh," Jane said. "Right now, I have nowhere to put them. Nowhere to live right now."

She thinly smiled, Richard noted.

Richard watched the sunny smile fade away to nothing and Jane's shoulders slump down. He wanted to rush over to her and draw her into his arms and, no, he had to stop the fantasy starting to take root in his brain and become the staid, somewhat stodgy, but ever reliable man he is known to be. "I will send a wagon."

Mr. Miller looked up and Jane frowned, confusion evident in the expression on her face.

"Miss Smith and I are affianced, and I will bring her belongings here. We will be wed as soon as the banns are read for the required Sundays."

Mr. Miller beamed. "I always did like a happy ending" he said and added "Miss Smith can come and stay with my family until the wedding day."

"Thank you, but she will remain here. My mother is her chaperone." *And my sisters,* for nothing got past his sisters. They would have made the spies in the war against France look pathetic if they had been a member of that elite group of British spies, The Kings Men, he thought.

"No one asked me how *I* feel" Jane said, misery evident in every word. The defeated look on her face bore testimony to her feelings.

"Well, of course we shall be wed as soon as may be," Richard said. "You are wearing my ring."

"It was a ruse. You said," Jane stated, before she was interrupted.

Mr. Miller spoke then. "Miss Smith is a relative of mine and I will take responsibility for her. She will come to live with me until she decides what she wants to do in the future. Would that suit you, Miss Smith?"

Sir Richard frowned. He was not used to people gainsaying him. He opened his mouth to protest when his mother said, a hint of laughter in her voice "That would be most appropriate, Mr. Miller, for you to provide a home for Miss Smith, who is, after all, a member of your family."

Mr. Miller turned to Jane, who stood near him, her handkerchief twisted into knots,

"Please come join my family and stay for as long as you wish. Miller Hall has many empty guest rooms and suites. I think you will be most comfortable. And you will meet many of your mother's family who live in the area."

Jane just stood there, and, said nothing.

SIR RICHARD MEETS HIS MATCH

"Please. Say yes, Miss Smith, please join my family. You can stay as long as you wish."

"Oh, I would love that above all else" she said, casting an unreadable look at Sir Richard.

"We will leave as soon as you are ready." Mr. Miller said, as Sir Richard glowered.

"I have nothing of my own" Jane said, quietly. Everything was left at the cottage."

"Everything from the cottage has been transported to my estate and will be available to you," her cousin said, smiling.

"Feel free to keep the dresses and clothing the girls gave you" Sir Richard's mother quickly said. "The girls have more gowns than they need."

Jane smiled at her.

Then Richard pulled the ribbon to summon Sims, and all was controlled confusion as maids were summoned to pack all of the clothing, despite Jane's protests that surely the girls would want some of those pretty gowns back.

In short order Jane was being assisted on with her cloak and bonnet and embraced by all of the girls and their mother. Last of Richard found himself looking down at Jane's very solemn face.

He wanted to beg her to stay. He clasped her hands in his and wished her well. That was it and then her cousin was tucking her hand through his arm and walking her to the front door.

He did not want to see her leave. He headed to his office while his mother and sisters fare-welled her. Part way up the stairs, he stopped and then returned to see her off. He joined his family on the front steps.

He could not wave, He felt bereft. As if his best friend in the world had left him. *What does that mean?* He wanted to shout to the coachman to stop the horses. He said nothing, his hands at his side. He felt alone, even though his whole family was right beside him.

I was used to her being here. I will not miss her for long. He would make himself forget her.

Chapter 29

Jane found herself torn between staying with Sir Richard and his family and going to live with her mother's cousin and his family.

"It was a ruse. You said," Jane stated, drawing a slow breath, trying not to faint for her heart was beating so fast, most likely from excitement, that she felt a little faint. She was hopeful that Sir Richard really wanted to wed her and dreaded the thought that he was just being kind. *I want him to love me. I do not want pity. I want him to marry me because he wants to not because he feels sorry for me. I must get away from him. I can not bear to have him pity me.*

She turned toward Mr. Miller.

"Please come join my family and stay for as long as you wish. Miller

Hall has many empty guest rooms and suites. I think you will be very comfortable. And you will meet many of your mother's family who live in the area."

Jane just stood there, saying nothing, but thinking how wonderful it would be to meet her mother's family, yet she knew she would miss this family, Sir Richard in particular. *Is this what love is?*

"Please. Say yes, Miss Smith, please join my family. You can stay as long as you wish."

"Oh, I would love that above all else" she said, looking over at Sir Richard.

"We will leave as soon as you are ready." Mr. Miller said, as Sir Richard glowered.

"Feel free to keep the dresses and clothing the girls gave you" Sir Richard's mother quickly said. "The girls have more gowns than they need."

Jane smiled at her in gratitude. Mayhap she would take a few with her. *They are so much prettier than the drab day dresses I wore at home at the cottage.*

Then Sir Richard pulled the ribbon to summon Sims and all was controlled confusion as maids were summoned to pack all of the clothing, despite Jane's protests that surely the girls would want some of those pretty gowns back, and almost before she knew, it she was being assisted on with her cloak and bonnet and embraced by all of the girls and their mother and last of all she found herself looking up into the very solemn face of Sir Richard himself.

His face was unreadable. He looked so handsome and so dear. Her heart sank for he did not beg her to stay. He clasped her hands in his and wished her well. That was it and then her cousin was tucking her hand through his arm and walking her to the front door.

Cousin William handed her up into his carriage and bade her to sit in the forward-facing seat and then seated himself across from her.

Sally followed them into the coach, as was proper. She would return after Jane had properly arrived at Cousin William's home.

Jane glanced out of the window as the driver gave the horses the office. Sir Richard stood at the top of the front steps with his mother and sisters. They were all waving to her. She waved back.

It did not escape her attention that Sir Richard was not among those waving.

He just stared at the carriage, his hands at his side. Again, she could not see any emotion on his face. *He will not miss me.*

She was sure now that she would never see him again and her heart broke in two. *Can one die of a broken heart?*

Sally had followed her into the coach, as was proper. She would be returned here at a later time.

Jane was happy to have Sally continue to be her maid for the short term, while she got acquainted with her new family and home.

Chapter 30

Jane awoke early in the morning after coming to Miller Hall. She stood at the window as the sky lightened. The sun would be rising very shortly. She liked the sunrise, always had. When she was younger, she anticipated a day of learning new things with her parents. Her father liked to look for old coins and pottery and her mother liked to read about faraway places. She idly traced the frost patterns on the glass of the window with her finger. *I was lucky to have such wonderful parents, how can I go on alone now?*

And today is Christmas Day and I have no gifts for the family.

A few minutes later a cheerful Sally was bringing her hot chocolate and laying out her clothing for the day.

Then Jane went down to breakfast and found the Millers there, with their very sweet daughter, Anne, who said she had always wanted a sister.

Mr. Miller said he felt bad about turning her out of her home. Both Mr. and Mrs. Miller said they wanted to do everything they could to make it up to her, including making sure she met the rest of her mother's family. A welcoming party for early in the year was in the planning stages. Epiphany was not that far away, Jane was told at the breakfast table.

Today would be a busy day with gifts for the servants and the tenants to be distributed. Jane was invited to join in and she eagerly accepted. The family, as with Sir Richard's family, kept to the old German traditions and celebrated family gift exchanges on Epiphany, she was told.

Everything from the cottage had been brought here for storage. She could, at leisure, sort through her mother's things. Her father's books were already shelved in the library. She still had Sir Richard's ring. He had forbidden her to return it to him. She had wrapped some string around and around it to keep it from falling off of her finger.

Even with the long coach ride and then the late Christmas Eve church service, Jane had had difficulty sleeping the previous night. She dreamt of him. He kissed her and she was so happy and then he turned his back and walked away. Jane awoke with tears running down her face.

And here she was tracing frost patterns on the glass window and asking herself the question, *do I love him?* She did not know. She only knew that she missed him. *And I miss his kiss,* she thought that morning as the first rays of the sun made the ice on the trees sparkle like a fairy land. She blushed at the thought of him kissing her even though there was no one to see.

The next day after nuncheon, Cousin Will, as he told her to call him, even though it was her mother who was his first cousin, sent Jane into the village with his mother and their daughter, Anne, to purchase gifts. "I am sure there are a few things you will wish to get for yourself and perhaps something for Sir Richard and his family for Epiphany" he said, a smile on his face. He gave her a purse with some coins. "It's the least I can do," he said by explanation and would not take them back. His smile was genuine, and Jane felt relieved to not be penniless.

So Jane purchased lace edged handkerchiefs for each of the girls, a pretty, lacy cap for his mother, and for Sir Richard she drew a blank. What to get him? There was nothing to be had there. She purchased gifts for the Millers next, but still could not find anything suitable for Sir. Richard.

She then went to the shop next door. She would be lost if there was nothing there for there were only two shops in the village. Then she saw it. A beautiful painting. It was by a local artist and showed a valley with the sun just peeking over the hill. There was glistening snow as it was a winter scene and down in the valley, way below, a sleigh could be seen being pulled by a matched pair of bays. She was so sure he would really like it. She could just picture it on the wall in his cottage in the woods. She would bring it back and ask Mr. Miller to send these items on to Sir Richard and his family. She counted out the coins in her purse and was pleased to find she had enough to pay for the painting.

She missed the family at Winslow Hall. She missed *him*. She sighed and decided to count her blessings. She had no illusions. She could have died in the brook. And as for Sir Richard? *He is a kind man, but he really does not want to have me for a wife. He would not have let me go if he did. It is time to face reality. He does not want me.* The tears started to course down her cheeks. Jane dabbed at her cheeks with her handkerchief and after paying for the painting and making arrangements for it to be delivered to the sleigh, she left to look for Mrs. Miller.

That afternoon at tea she asked Mrs. Miller about wrapping the gifts in paper and sending them on to Sir Richard's home.

Mrs. Miller smiled, saying that the day after Epiphany will be just fine.

The days sped by.

Chapter 31

Epiphany is tomorrow; she thought as she climbed into bed and blew out the candle.

The night seemed long. Jane tossed half the night and finally fell into a fitful sleep. Now as the maid, Nell was scratching on the door to come in and help her get ready for the day she thought about the day and remembered her happy life before her parents died. She sighed.

She had a gift for each of the Millers: a pretty shawl for Mrs. Miller, a bit of Belgian lace for their daughter, Anne, and a book on Roman coins for Mr. Miller after he had expressed an interest in them.

The day was a festive occasion, and Jane tried to get into a festive mood. She smiled and laughed - a bit forced perhaps, but it was the best she could do. It felt like her face would crack at times. She found herself wondering about Sir Richard and was picturing him and his mother and sisters in their cozy parlour opening gifts. *How I wish I were there*. Jane sighed, apparently loudly, because Mrs. Miller gave her an odd look.

The Millers expressed appreciation for her gifts and pronouncing them all to be quite wonderful, in turn gave her some gifts with smiles and there was something else. It was as if they were expecting something or knew something that Jane was not aware of. No one said anything, but there was an air of expectation and every time there was a noise from outside Jane noticed at least one of them would look toward the window which looked out drive to the barn.

Jane was given a deep rose wool gown and also a warm cloak to wear which pleased her immensely. Her old cloak was quite shabby and the worse for wear after its dunking in the brook. Also, they gave her beautiful half boots for there was snow on the ground and Jane's boots were rather worn and shabby. And a reticle as well, complete with a handkerchief embroidered with a blue bird, tucked inside. She smiled, thanked them soundly for they are such beautiful and thoughtful gifts. And, she was sure, the bird had been embroidered by Mrs. Miller.

The tears in her eyes must have spoken volumes, for the Millers laughed and arising went to where she was and took turns hugging her and wishing her a Happy Christmas.

Suddenly Jane felt like she belonged. This is my family; Jane thought to herself and laughed out loud. "I have a home now," she said aloud.

"Jane, you are our family, and you will always have a home with us, come what may," Mr. Miller told her, and Mrs. Miller agreed, a smile on her face.

Just then someone dropped the knocker on the door. And a few minutes later the butler announced the arrival of Sir Richard Winslow. Mr. Miller asked to have Sir Richard shown in.

And then he was there, standing in the doorway and if it was possible, Jane's heart turned over. He looked wonderful. His smile was warm as he turned to face her. He murmured a greeting, but Jane was so overcome with emotion she could not focus on what he was saying. Something about a wedding and then he was there in front of her and then he was sitting next to her, and the rest of the room faded away until it was as if it was just the two them in their own private world.

He cupped her face and looked deep into her eyes. "My dear. My dearest darling Jane," he began as beyond them the other occupants of the room made themselves scarce and left them alone in the parlour. Not even a maid was left for proprietary reasons. There are advantages to being engaged, even a sham engagement, Jane thought as she looked up into Sir Richard's eyes and he smiled. Her breath hitched and her hands started to tremble. When he removed his hands, she felt bereft.

Jane was shaking with an emotion she could not identify. *He is here. The man she knew she could never have, yet never live without.* Wordlessly she arose and went to retrieve the package she had wrapped to have sent over to his home.

After she climbed the stairs and entered the sitting room, she hardly noticed the smiling family members sitting in front of the fire drinking tea and chatting. She picked up the package, belatedly noticed everyone, sent a quick smile in their direction, returned to the parlour and handed the package to him.

Sir Richard took the package and said simply, "For me?"

Jane nodded, unable to speak.

He carefully took it out of the paper and stared at it. "It is perfect," he said, simply, "like you."

"Sir Richard" Jane said, "I have been so,"

"Hush, my darling, let me finish, I beg of you."

She was puzzled when he took his ring off of her finger. It took a little doing because the string made it so snug. *Well, that answers that question. He does not want to marry me,* she thought, as her finger felt empty without the ring.

Her heart broke into little pieces, and she wanted to cry. Yes, she had refused him, but she had hoped, oh, she had hoped that he would see through her need to protect her heart and insist that he loved her. Well, I should have known better, she thought, as a tear slid down her cheek. Turning her face away from him so that he could not see it, she swiped at the offending tear as unobtrusively as she could.

"Go now, Sir Richard," she said as soon as she was able to regain a measure of calmness and self-control. She did not want to turn into a watering pot just because he wanted to end their betrothal.

After all, she had tried to turn him down. She wanted to make the ending of their sham betrothal as easy for him as possible.

"Go now, Sir Richard" she said, again, and walked out of the room.

He stood there, his mouth agape.

Chapter 32

Jane's cousin then entered the room.

"I think I have caused Miss Smith to misunderstand my intentions" Sir Richard said and explained the situation to the Millers, as Mrs. Miller had joined them.

"I think she is in love with you, Sir Richard" Mrs. Miller said, "but I think she needs a little time to think things through clearly. She has had quite an ordeal."

"I agree with you, Mrs. Miller" he said and a few minutes later Sir Richard found himself being shown out.

On the ride home he felt bereft as if he had lost his best friend and a part of himself.

The next morning Sir Richard decided to seek the consul of his mother, who had dealt with the loss of her own husband at a relatively young age and who is always a font of intelligent information and ideas.

"You need to court her, my son" she said, smiling. "She is young and deserves to be courted."

"Courted? But I already proposed. What else should I do?"

"Send her some flowers. We have some in bloom in the conservatory."

"Flowers? Oh, I did not think of that."

"I will write to the Millers and invite all of them for supper and they can stay for a few days here. There is an assembly next week and I am sure they will be happy to attend. They have a daughter who will be making her come-out next spring."

Chapter 33

"Marry me, my precious angel. Marry me soon."

"What?" Jane breathed, afraid to believe that he had said the words she wanted to hear. Words he said because he wanted to marry her for herself, not just to save her from destitution.

He reached for her, and as he put his arms around her to kiss her, she woke up with a start.

It was all a dream. A stupid dream. She sat up in bed and wanted to cry. *I love him and I can not have him. And I will not let him marry me out of pity.*

She rolled over in her big, lonely bed and tried to go back to sleep. Eventually exhaustion won out and she slept in fits and starts.

A footman arrived the next afternoon with an invitation to spend a few days with Sir Richard and his family, for there would be an assembly held at the local hall during the week of the visit.

The Millers were delighted. "This way Anne can practice her steps with the local lads prior to her come out in the spring," Mrs. Miller said. "And we are sure that you would be happy to see Sir Richard's family as well, Jane" Mr. Miller added.

Of course, she would, but she was not sure what to make of the huge bouquet of hot house flowers that the footman had brought along specifically for her. There was another bouquet, a little smaller, for Anne. Jane smiled. Sir Richard is a kind man. Many men would not have thought to send a bouquet to the other young lady. The note read "To Jane. Far lovelier than any flower" and it was signed by Sir Richard. Anne's flowers were accompanied by a note as well wishing her happiness in this a new year.

"It looks like you have a suitor" Mrs. Miller said as she read the note after Jane handed it to her."

"Whatever do you mean?" Jane asked.

Mrs. Miller only smiled.

Later, as they were walking to the dining room, Mrs. Miller said to her husband, "Sir Richard is courting our Miss Smith."

"I thought he would come up to scratch" he said as he leaned over and kissed her, right there in the middle of the hallway.

"Someone will see," she protested weakly, and he laughed.

Chapter 34

Time passed quickly as the Millers prepared to go to stay with Sir Richard's family for a few days.

A ball gown had to be made for Jane for she had had none. It was light blue as she was old enough not to have to wear white as a debutante would. There was a blue sash as well that was nearly the color of her eyes. She could not wait for the night of the assembly to wear it.

And, she had to admit to herself, it was not the assembly and dancing that was attracting her, but Sir Richard. She could not wait to see him again.

And then, finally, it was time to go. The trip there seemed endless, and it was all she could do not to ask if they were almost there.

And then they were progressing up the long drive. Snow still lingered and she could hear it crunch beneath the feet of the horses pulling the coach and she could feel her heart hammering in her chest. *I can not wait to see him again.*

And then there they were in front of the Hall and there he was standing on the top step, waiting for them. For her? She hoped. *Oh, Good Lord, I hope. I wish.*

He walked to the coach and waited while Tom, a footman, helped the family down the steps. When it was her turn, Sir Richard, himself, helped her out and tucking her hand under his arm led them all up the stairs and into the Hall where his mother and sisters waited to greet everyone.

He bowed, correctly, over her hand and then they were all talking at once and everyone was smiling.

She glanced up at his face. He looked quite serious. She could not read his thoughts.

Tea and scones were served. And after everyone had freshened up a magnificent supper was served in the dining room with Jane seated to his right and his mother at the foot of the table as was usual, Mr. Howard to her left.

Then tea was served in the drawing room.

Sir Richard spoke to her cousin and his wife and their daughter, Anne. Then he sat next to Jane and asked about her life with her cousin's family.

All too soon it was time to go to their bedrooms and Sir Richard walked to his office with her cousin. It was as if the sun had vanished when he walked away. She missed his touch. She felt a chill. *Will my life be filled with joy the few times in a year when I see him and bleakness when he walks away?*

Sally escorted her to her room. Hers was the room she had stayed in when she had first come there, and it was nice to be there in that familiar place. She smiled when she saw a bouquet of flowers on the small table next to the bed.

In his office, Sir Richard and Cousin Miller had a long discussion, which ended cordially with the two men shaking hands in agreement.

Richard was encouraged by all he heard from the cousin.

Jane had settled in with the family and was happy enough but mentioned Richard's name often enough that the Miller's felt she missed him.

The Millers were amenable to him offering for her.

The cousin urged restraint initially until the time felt right. Richard knew it would be difficult to do but he would do whatever he needed to do to win her over.

Chapter 35

The days passed quickly as the family had many quiet entertainments planned for them.

Nightly there were guests from the village and surrounding areas, so the Hall was filled each evening with voices and laughter.

Charades one night and a night of music with one of his sisters playing the pianoforte and another on the harp another night. Cards on yet another with Sir Richard as her partner.

Oh, I wish this week will never end, she found herself thinking on the third night as she climbed into a bed that had been warmed with a warming pan.

Then came the night of the assembly and they were bundled into sleighs with warm bricks at their feet as there was still snow on the ground and the air was very cold outside. Heavy robes, muffs for their hands and warm bonnets kept them from being chilled.

Sir Richard asked for the first dance, a quadrille, and signed her card. She noted he also signed her card in two other places. Certain that it was a mistake she started to say something as she pointed out the three places.

He was quiet for a very long moment and then he said, "No. I did not make a mistake," and he walked away. Gaping, she looked after him. Dancing three sets in one night with the same woman was the same as a declamation of the intent to marry. Could it be? Could he be making his feelings known in such a public way? She sought out Mrs. Miller and explained her dilemma.

"Dance with him" she advised. "He is a man and knows his own mind." And she smiled.

So Jane did. She danced the quadrille and a reel and then came the supper dance and she thought she would die of happiness. He was smiling at her, and she decided to just enjoy the evening and worry about nothing. *I know he would never deliberately hurt me, so I am going to trust in him*, she thought, as he bowed over her hand at the end of the last set.

And then they had supper with several of his friends and she hoped the night would never end.

They are so nice to me, she thought as all they laughed and ate and laughed some more.

All too soon it was time to return to the Hall and they piled into sleighs. Sir Richard sat next to her this time and held her hand under the blanket. He squeezed her hand and asked her if she had had a nice evening.

"Oh, but I have," she said, as she smiled. The night sky was full of stars and the snow crunched under the hooves of the horses' feet and her hand, snug in Sir Richard's, was warm. She felt safe. And she was happy. She thought *I will let tomorrow take care of itself. Tonight, I am happy.*

Chapter 36

Sir Richard thought that Jane had never looked lovelier. The sash of her gown matched her eyes. Her hair was swept up on her head in a mass of curls and blue ribbon. She was wearing the ear bobs and necklace that had belonged to her mother. When he first saw her, his breathing hitched for a moment. He had wanted to take her home to his bed and claim her for himself. He had taken a slow breath to steady himself.

She protested the place on her card where he had not put his name, not twice, but three times. Mayhap she had not realized he was making a very public statement of his regard for her. She danced with him, all three dances, and smiled and laughed through all of them.

Jane also seemed to like his friends. He caught sight of her smiling and conversing easily with them.

In conversations with his friends during the rest of the dance after supper, he found that they all liked her. They all stated that they felt that Jane had a special regard for him.

That night he had difficulty falling asleep. He wanted to hold her, kiss her and love her.

Chapter 37

The next day right after nuncheon, Richard, looking quite solemn asked her to join him in the small parlour. His mother, serving as chaperone, was seated out in the hallway.

He led Jane into the room and then, against all convention, closed the door. She expected his mother to open the door at any moment and she expectantly looked that way but that did not happen.

They were standing in the middle of the room. The sun outside shone in the windows and left a patch of sunlight on the carpet.

She bowed her head body. She blushed deeply.

Sir Richard wondered out loud what maggot had buried itself in her brain.

Instead of taking offense she blushed furiously.

He frowned for a moment.

"Tell me?" he asked, as he placed one finger under her chin and tipped her chin up.

She shook her head and started laughing.

"You will, you know."

"I will what?"

"You will tell me when you are ready."

"No, I will not" she protested, tears now running down her face from laughter…

"You will," he insisted, "If not now, then sometime in the next year or so. I am nothing, if not persistent. I always get my way." And a smile lit his face.

"Marry me," he said, with no preamble, no poetic verses, and no romantic gestures.

Just a simple demand, for he was not asking. He had already done that, and it had come to naught.

Chapter 38

I love him, she thought, and almost cried for they would be leaving for the Millers home soon. *I do not want to go away from him.*

They were standing in the middle of the room. The sun outside shone in the windows and left a patch of sunlight on the carpet. *This is where we stood, before,* Jane noted.

She bowed her head. She was not sure what he was going to say. *Is it possible he is being so nice to me because he feels sorry for me? Or that he feels obligated because of what had happened at the cottage? As if anyone would believe that nothing had happened. Well, being stripped naked is something, that is true.* She blushed at the thought that he had seen her naked body. Strange, she had not thought about that before and she blushed even more deeply.

Sir Richard wondered out loud what maggot had buried itself in her brain.

Instead of taking offense she blushed furiously.

He frowned for a moment.

"Tell me?" he asked, as he placed one finger under her chin and tipped her chin up.

She shook her head and started laughing.

"You will, you know."

"I will what?"

"You will tell me when you are ready."

"No, I will not" she protested, tears now running down her face from laughter...

"You will," he insisted, "If not now, then sometime in the next year or so. I am nothing, if not persistent. I always get my way." And a smile lit his face.

"Marry me," he said, with no preamble, no poetic verses, and no romantic gestures.

Jane was not insulted by the demand, but she was stunned. It was not the words, but the intensity of them and the look on his face. A look of raw hunger and need.

She stepped back. He let go of her hands as she did. *Could this be? Could he mean it? Really want me? For myself?*

Jane then spoke. "But, I have no title, no distinguished family. I am destitute, I am..."

"Marry me, sweet Jane. Please make my life complete and be my wife."

"But..." Jane said as he stepped forward and embraced her. He looked down into her eyes.

"I care not about your family. I care not about your past. I want you, my love, I, well, I need you in my life. Please. Dear Jane. Make me the happiest of men and marry me."

Jane looked up into his eyes, stunned. *He* wants *to marry me*, she thought and smiled up at him.

"Yes. Oh, yes" Jane exclaimed and the next thing she knew he had taken her in his arms and was kissing her as if there was nothing else he wanted to do.

A few minutes later they parted. He took her left hand in his and slid on a beautiful ring of the prettiest blue sapphire she had ever seen.

"I think the color matches your eyes," he said, "or as close as I could get it," he finished.

"I think it is lovely" Jane said, and tears again dampened her cheeks but this time they were tears of joy. "Are you sure that you really want to marry me?" Jane asked.

"I can not sleep. I think of you when I should be working on my estate books. I have no appetite. I am lovesick, my dearest. I confess, I desire you, I want you. I... I love you."

"Oh, Sir Richard, I love you too."

"Call me Richard, dearest."

"What?"

"Call me Richard, dearest. Please."

"Yes," she said simply.

"Shall we tell the Millers you have agreed to make me the happiest of men?"

"I truly hope Sir, that is, Richard. I want to make you happy for the rest of our lives."

Chapter 39

In the main hallway, Sir Richard Winslow, known for his impeccable manners and perfect deportment, did the unthinkable. With no mistletoe in sight, he still kissed his bride-to-be in front of several footmen and maids and he did not care. Even with his smiling mother looking on he did not care. *I need her in my life*, he thought, as Jane looked around the hall and then blushed.

Jane is going to be mine in every way. He wanted to shout it from the top of the nearest hill. Sir Richard settled for announcing it at supper that evening, with Jane seated next to him and smiling broadly.

The Millers were delighted, and his sisters were over the moon with excitement.

Even the butler was smiling. He saw his mother quietly grasp the hand of Mr. Howard.

Chapter 40

Now Jane was back with the Millers preparing for their wedding.

His mother and sisters were busy sprucing up the already clean Hall.

His mother moved out of the rooms she had shared with his father and into another suite of rooms. She was having the master suite refurbished for him and his bride.

When Richard protested, she firmly said, "It is time I did. This is time for your bride to take up the reins of being in charge of her own household. I will be happy to teach her everything she needs to know."

"But…" was as far as he got when she continued "She will need guidance. It is time."

His mother then turned and left him standing in the middle of the breakfast room as she left the room.

His sisters were over the moon about the up-coming wedding and many trips were made to the village seamstress for the fittings. Three gowns to be made up in short order meant that the village seamstress needed more helpers. A boon for her daughters who often helped her when she was busy.

The weeks passed in a haze of excitement and impatience as Sir Richard and his family waited to have the banns read starting the next Sunday.

Chapter 41

The Millers had the village seamstress make up a dress of a shade of blue to match Jane's eyes and a new pale green color gown for Anne to wear as well. Anne was to be Jane's only attendant.

Jane loved her new dress. It was lovely, with an overlay of lace and a reticle and a fan to match.

Time crawled by.

Finally, the day arrived. They went by coach, there not being enough snow for a sleigh.

They arrived at the church. Butterflies fluttered through her midsection as Cousin Miller handed her out of the coach. Mrs. Miller and Anne had been helped out of the coach and then had immediately gone into the church, Anne waiting just inside the door.

Cousin Miller set her hand on his sleeve, and, giving her a smile, they headed up the walk to the church.

"Nervous?"

"Yes," she breathed.

"You look lovely. Sir Richard is a lucky man."

She carried herself with pride up the front steps of the local church. She felt secure with her cousin there with her.

Then they were progressing down the aisle, Jane just ahead of her.

The village church was filled, she could see, as they walked. She saw the servants from the Millers estate and then everyone she had met in the village. Even the seamstress who had made her dress was there, a happy smile on her face, along with her grinning daughters. The youngest one gave a little wave.

Jane nearly waved back before stopping herself.

Mrs. Miller was in the front pew, a newly embroidered handkerchief in her hands as tears glistened on her cheeks.

Sir Winslow's family was there too, his mother smiling mistily, Mr. Howard at her side, and Sir Winslow's sister, Lilly, giggling as usual, and Holly, who was looking forward to her come out next Season, sitting there in perfect decorum. No doubt practicing a little restraint in preparation for spring.

And there ahead of her, his eyes alight with love and a smile of welcome on his face was Sir Richard. He reached out and took her hand and then Cousin William left her there and went to sit with Mrs. Miller in the front row.

She hardly heard the words. She recited her vows, and she remembered signing the book afterward with her new name. The rest was a happy blur.

Then they climbed into coaches and headed back to Miller Hall for a wedding breakfast. Everyone from the village had been invited and it was a few hours before the happy couple could get away and head for Sir Richard's home, which was only a few hours' drive away.

"The poor horses must be tired" Jane remarked as they started off.

"Oh, I have your cousin's horses" Richard said. "I am sure we will be back to visit soon, and we can just switch out horses again."

You think of everything, Sir Richard," Jane said.

"Richard, dearest Jane."

"What?"

"Please, call me Richard, dearest wife."

Jane laughed. "Yes, Richard. I will Richard. I will be a good wife, Richard. But I might call you Sir Richard if I am vexed."

"You do not take direction well, dear wife," Sir Richard said.

And then they both laughed.

Chapter 42

Jane marveled at the beautiful room she was shone into by her maid, Sally. "How beautiful, this is perfect for us."

"My lady, this is your room. Sir Richard's room is beyond that door, and behind this door on the other side is your private parlour, wardrobe and bathing chamber."

"We have separate bedrooms?"

"Yes, my lady, this is the way the upper class live."

"Oh. My. I did not know."

This elicited a sympathetic look from Sally, who then briskly changed the subject by suggesting they look in her wardrobe for her dinner dress and then that she take a short nap. Sally would bring her some tea in an hour's time.

Jane thanked her and said she would like to think about dressing for dinner after her nap.

Sally protested she would not have time to properly press her dress, but Jane sent her a look that sent Sally out of the room with no more protest after assisting Jane out of her dress and into the most comfortable bed Jane had ever slept in.

Jane knew she would not sleep and was startled awake by a warm arm over her and her face being covered with kisses.

"What, Oh, Ah"

SIR RICHARD MEETS HIS MATCH

"Sorry to awaken you so abruptly, but I wished to finish what we started in the coach."

"Oh, Yes," Jane said and blushed deeply.

When Sally returned with the cup of tea and a few biscuits, Richard, as he asked Jane to call him, had returned to his own room, after making a simple request to ask Sally to ask the cook to have their supper delivered to Jane's private parlour.

Sally placed the cup on the stand at the side of the bed. As it was drawing dark, she lit the candle there and the one on the mantle, and then added more wood to the fire.

"As soon as you have finished your tea, we should choose your gown for..."

"I am so sorry, Sally, I have no need to change for supper as Sir Richard and I wish to have supper in my parlour. Will that be a problem?"

"No, I will inform Cook. Do you wish to change into something more comfortable for supper?"

"Yes, Sally," she said and blushed. She realized the rumpled bed told its own story.

After Sally and Jane had chosen a simple yet attractive dress from her wardrobe and Jane had been helped into it, Sally left to consult with the cook.

Jane decided to look through the wardrobe and see what other surprises were in there. The dress she was now wearing had never been part of her very limited wardrobe. Her closet was now filled with dresses, most she had never seen before.

Jane was standing there frowning when a shadow fell over her, and turning she saw Richard walking through the doorway.

"You look perplexed, my dearest."

"Richard, there are dresses here I have never seen before. They can not be mine."

"My dearest, they are yours. My mother, I see, has been diligently adding to your wardrobe. Do not worry, I will speak with her."

"She is ashamed of me."

"No, my dearest, she cares about you and wants you to be comfortable in clothing that is considered the usual style of dress for one in our position in society. Nevertheless, I will speak with her."

"Oh."

Richard turned and strode out of the room at the sound of a tap on the outer parlour door.

Jane followed him. "Oh, I did not realize the parlour has its own door to the hallway."

Richard smiled. "You will get used to it, my dear. Do not fret."

Several footmen brought in food and serving ware and set a table using a white tablecloth.

Richard seated Jane and took his seat across from her. They waited while the footmen served them and filled their wine glasses, and being thanked, departed, leaving them alone with a nice fire in the parlour fireplace and candles lit on the mantle and on the center of the table. It was cozy and intimate.

Exactly what we need, Jane thought. *I need to take charge of how I will go on, tonight, or do what Richard and his mother want me to do.* She took a breath and then told Richard how she felt and what she was planning on doing.

She watched his face closely. He frowned, he beetled his eyebrows, he looked perplexed, and he looked quite worried for a bit. She finished her piece, as she finished her meal, and waited for him to comment. He did not. She watched his face become expressionless and then he smiled, and she then knew it was going to be all right.

"It will be as you wish" he said.

She watched him stand and come around the table and reach down and then he drew her up into his arms.

"Come my dear wife. Let us go to bed."

"Where?" she asked, now her turn to look perplexed.

"Why, my bed of course. It is much larger."

"Oh" is all she could think to say.

Chapter 43

Sir Richard was working on his estate books. Or so he had planned for this afternoon. He found himself, instead, staring out of the window and thinking obsessively about Jane. He wondered if she was finished with her planned meeting with the housekeeper and the cook yet. Perhaps they could spend a few hours before supper in his bed.

Untutored as she was, she was a quick learner and he had so much he wanted to teach her.

His thoughts were interrupted by a scratching on the door. "Open," he called.

His mother walked in. His mouth dropped open as he sadly realized his afternoon romp would now have to be postponed until this evening.

"Mother, I, that is, we, did not expect you for five more days."

"Well, dearest," his mother replied, "I realized that Jane would need help in running the household so I thought we should return, posthaste."

"Oh. Well, as to that, your training of the staff, ah, has sustained us so you can return and enjoy your stay at her cousin's home for the rest of your planned visit."

"Posh, I can not do that to poor Jane. Where is she? Perhaps in her sitting room? I do hope she likes the way I decorated her rooms for her. They were in need of refurbishing."

"As to that, Mother. She noticed the extra clothing. I am perfectly capable of clothing my own wife."

His mother just shrugged. She was used to getting her own way. "Where is she? I wish to help her get used to running a household. And we need to talk about her chickens while we are at it. They are pets, Richard. Can you believe that? They all have names."

Richard laughed. Yes, he could believe that. Jane had lived alone in a cottage and counted on the eggs her hens laid to keep her in food for herself and for bartering. Of course, she had named them. She likely even talked to them, like she did to Dusty.

As his mother turned towards the door, Richard spoke up. "Why not wash the dust of travel off and have a cup of tea in the back parlour. When Jane is finished with her meeting, I am sure she will be happy to join you there for tea."

"Meeting? What meeting?" his mother asked.

"With our housekeeper and cook. Do not interfere, Mother," he warned.

His mother, of course, did not heed his instructions. He heard her ask their butler where Jane was. He almost wished he could be there because he felt one of them, his mother or Jane, would have very hurt feelings and he was not sure which one it would be.

His mother, of course, was used to running this household for well over 25 years. Yet, she had told Jane that it was time to turn over management to her and had handed over her chatelaine. Now Jane had the keys to everything in the Hall and the authority. *Will she give it back?* Richard was not sure that Jane would, yet, his mother could be quite a force to be reckoned with at times. *Is this one of those times.*

Chapter 44

Jane swallowed, took a deep breath and walked into the back parlour. This was to be her first meeting with the housekeeper and the cook, and she understood that you can only make one first good impression.

The first thing she had done was to establish a time. Then she asked the cook to have a maid bring them the tea cart just before their meeting. When she saw the smile on the cook's face, she knew she had made a good first decision. She took another deep breath and awaited her guests. The cook arrived with the maid who brought the tea trolley. The housekeeper walked in right after them.

As they seated themselves Jane started pouring cups of tea for each of them at the table she had had set up in the center of the room. She gave both the cook and the housekeeper a cup of tea.

From the smiles on their faces and their responses, she felt like she was on the verge of establishing a good working relationship with them. Jane remembered that as a child her mother would tell her to always treat people with respect, no matter their class in society. "Treat others as you wish to be treated," her mother often said.

She asked them what they needed. It seemed there were no needs. All was supplied when required and they were happy.

It was at that point that her mother-in-law walked in, a smile on her face.

Jane swallowed too fast and almost choked on her tea. *What should I do now? I have to establish myself as mistress here.*

Her mother-in- law turned to get a chair for herself and Jane quickly said "I am so sorry, my lady, but we are having a private meeting just now."

Her mother-in-law froze, her hands gripping the chair, her mouth open in disbelief. She quickly closed her mouth and forced a smile.

Jane then said, "Let us meet in your sitting room when I am finished with my meeting."

Then her mother-in-law turned to Jane and said, "I will see you after your meeting, my dear." And she then quit the room.

For a few moments, no one said a word.

Then Jane asked, "What do wish for that you do not now have?" and the conversation opened once more. The cook wanted a kitchen garden that was larger than the small patch allotted to her now. Jane said that would be done as soon as the ground was ready for planting. The housekeeper was competent with herbs and wanted her own little patch in which to grow them. Jane then decided that the housekeeper would take over the cook's former garden patch and a new one would be established for the cook. Both stated that they were happy with that solution.

Jane told the housekeeper that she would have a duplicate chatelaine made up for her. The housekeeper thanked her profusely.

It was agreed that they would meet like this and discuss any problems with the running of the house over tea. It was also agreed that Jane would see each individually at regular intervals to make sure that all was running smoothly. She would keep Sir Richard apprised of any needs that were not being met.

Both the housekeeper and the cook thanked Jane for taking the time to meet with them over the tea table and that they are very happy to have her as their new mistress.

Jane then left the table and walked slowly to her mother-in-law's sitting room. She was not looking forward to seeing her mother-in-law again. Would she be angry at Jane? Would she even talk to her? She paused outside the door, tapped on it, drew in a deep breath, then eased the door open and walked in.

Chapter 45

Sir Richard again dipped his quill in the inkwell. His mother, at that point, entered his office and she was obviously unhappy. It looked like he was not going to get much done today,

"Yes, Mother, is all well with Jane?" he asked, as gently as he could, as his mother was frowning.

"I do not wish to discuss it, Richard. Please ring for tea."

Richard tried not to sigh. His books lay open, and he doubted he would have time to finish what he had started. Still, his mother looked troubled, and he knew he would have to resolve whatever was bothering her so much. Because something was.

"She does not need my help, Richard. I do not understand it."

"In what way, Mother? She has no experience in running a large house."

"And yet, all is running smoothly," she said and looked quite perplexed, as she wrung her hands in her lap.

Sir Richard thought for a moment. Then he smiled. "Of course, all is running smoothly, Mother. You trained the staff well. She will learn from them." And then he rose and pulled the bell cord. "I think a cup of tea is called for."

"Yes," she said, "No doubt, son, you are correct. I did train the staff well. But?"

"Yes, Mother. There is more?"

The butler arrived and a tea tray was ordered and then Sir Richard gently asked his mother what else was troubling her.

"She has all of these ideas."

"What kind of ideas?"

"She is planning on visiting the tenants to see how they are doing. She wants to have a fair on our grounds in the summer. She wants to start a class for the tenants and village children with the vicar. She plans to visit the vicarage and to visit the tenant families to see what our family can do to help them. Where did she learn how to do all of these things that I have been doing? Who told her? That is why I came back so early. I realized she would not know how to go on and now I found she does not need me. Where did she learn what is needed?"

Sir Richard laughed.

His mother frowned. "This is not something to joke about. Has she been lying to us all of this time about her upbringing?"

"Mother, she did not lie to us." His mother still looked concerned. "Jane lived in a humble cottage. She attended fairs at the home of the Marquis. She attended classes at the vicarage. She saw how the lady of the manor visited the poor and brought food and inquired into the needs of the families. Her cottage included. Her friends were the children of the shopkeepers and of the tenants of the Marquis. That is how she learned about the needs and wants of the local villagers. She lived that life.

"She comes from a good family. Her father was a scholar and not really interested in things. He is, was, well respected and was published in professional journals. There is not a great deal of money paid for those articles. She learned about old coins and pottery from him. She will be a great help for me, as I am interested in these things as well."

His mother said nothing. He could see she was thinking about what he said. Then he added, "I love her."

His mother smiled and then the tea trolley arrived. Richard asked the maid to ask her mistress to join them in his office. He looked quickly to see if there was any reaction from his mother over his referring to Jane as the mistress of the house.

She caught his look and smiled. *Good. Another hurdle surmounted.* He had been a little concerned how things would go on with two mistresses in the house.

Richard was astonished as his wife strode into the office as if it was her home to manage. He looked quickly at his mother, who was rising to her feet. He breathed a sigh of relief when his mother embraced Jane and said, "I can see that the house is in good hands, my dear. I will be returning to your cousin's house in a day or two. Would that be convenient?"

"Yes, My Lady," Jane answered.

"Mother, if you please," his mother said.

Jane smiled. "Yes, Mother. I will be looking forward to our making of plans for Holly's come out and how to keep Lily out of trouble."

His mother laughed and Sir Richard chuckled. Yes, Lily was always into mischief. Holly was more mature and level-headed. What most pleased him was the interplay between his mother and his wife. It looked like they would be able to get along well, after all.

They sipped tea in a companionable silence until his mother said, "We will be having a guest for supper." And said no more.

Richard thought it was likely that it would be her gentleman friend.

After Lily makes her debut in London next year, I may retire to the dower house," his mother said to them.

"No, Mother" both Sir Richard and Jane said at once.

"There is no more to be said. I plan on refurbishing it, come what may, once both girls are married and have homes of their own." Turning to Jane, she took her hand and said "You will do fine, my, uh, daughter. Do you mind if I call you daughter? You feel like one to me."

"Only if I may continue to call you Mother," Jane replied.

Both women were then crying and hugging, and Richard did not quite know what to do. So he pulled the cord and met Sims at the door and told him to tell the cook that there would be an extra guest for supper.

Remembering the way his mother had said she might retire to the dower house, Richard wondered if she was hoping that when Lily left the nest, he might come up to scratch. And if not, they would have more privacy there than they would have here. His mother deserved to be happy. All is well here. And he smiled.

Chapter 46

It was just before first light at Weatherby Hall.

In the night hours an owl hooted and a fox yipped.

In a quiet barn, a young groom watched over a mare, soon to foal.

A sleepy cook pulled a bell cord and returned to bed.

Then a stair creaked.

Lady Mary sat in the breakfast room sipping tea and wondering if she should stay or leave.

Someone quietly opened a door and silently slipped into a room.

A figure hovered momentarily over another person, the candle flame dancing from a faint draft.

Without warning, a scream shattered the stillness.

Chapter 47

Jane was jolted awake by a sharp pain on her shoulder and the horrified exclamation from her maid, Sally, who was standing over her.

Sir Richard awoke at the same time and protectively put his arm around her. It took a minute to sort everything out.

"Oh, I am so sorry, My Lady, I will get a cold cloth for your shoulder. Wax from my candle dripped on you."

Richard by that time had lit a candle on his side of the bed and had scooted back over to examine her shoulder, as Sally rushed in with a wet towel in her hand. "I am so sorry, Miss, Uh, Missus. The candle dripped wax on your shoulder."

Richard then said "It will be a bit sore for a few days, but no harm done, Sally. Why were you hovering over the bed?"

"I am so sorry. I did not know what to do. I believe Lady Winslow is leaving very early and thought you would like to know. I am sorry. Perhaps I should have waited, but she is dressed and sipping tea in the breakfast room."

Richard bit back a smile. Jane, as naked as the day she was born, was holding the sheet up to cover herself. *After all, Sally helped in the bath and helped her dress every day, yet Jane was shyly covering up as best as possible.*

Richard then spoke. "Sally, you say my mother is dressed and thinking of leaving? You did the right thing in telling us. Please pull the cord for my valet and help your mistress dress for the day."

After Jane and Sally had left, his valet walked into his room.

"Thompson, I need a shave and to dress for breakfast."

Thompson was a lackluster man, who asked no questions, but was always quick and thorough. Richard was washed, shaved and dressed before Jane was ready to go downstairs. He almost waited for her, but then decided a quiet discussion with his mother would likely be best, and he headed downstairs to the breakfast room.

Although it was early, when the cook heard the commotion from upstairs she had gotten out of bed and had quickly cooked breakfast.

His mother was eating eggs and toast when he walked in. He went to the sideboard and helped himself to toast and eggs. While passing up the kidneys, he took some bacon and sat down as a footman served him some tea.

"Well, Mother, what brings you to the breakfast table so early in the morning? Did you not sleep well last night?"

"I am not needed anymore. It is most vexing."

"Nonsense, Mother. You are the one who helped me win Jane over. You are the one who let her take over as mistress of Weatherby Hall and made sure she was able to do it on her own. You did the right thing. In the right way.

"The girls need you to guide them. Then during the next two years you will be busy helping Holly and then Lilly make their bows in London for the Season.

"And Jane is going to need your help in London. She has never been to a big city, let alone London."

He noted a smile on his mother's face.

"That I can do," she said. "But Richard…?"

"Yes, Mother?"

"She talks to her chickens like they are her children. She will not insist on taking them to London, will she?"

Richard laughed and was still laughing when Jane walked into the room. She was wearing one of the gowns his mother had gotten for her.

He saw his mother's face brighten when she recognized the gown.

He also saw approval on his mother's face as Jane's hair was now dressed in a more becoming style. *I will have to pay Sally a little more,* he thought. *She is learning how to manage Jane, in a good way.*

"Mother, I thought perhaps you and I could visit with the vicar today" Jane said, as she buttered her toast and then added some jam.

"I would be pleased to accompany you to the vicar's house" Richard's mother said, "before I leave for your cousin's home. I should return within a week with your, um, sisters."

Jane smiled. "I will look forward to seeing them come home."

Sir Richard smiled. *All is well in our world.*

A teaser for Book 2 of the Match series, "MisMatched"

The two families are preparing to go to London in order for Anne and Holly to make a match. Everything seems to be going smoothly. The girls, plus Lily, are practicing the piano and learning steps to the newest dances with a man they refer to as the "dancing master." Perhaps the hardest part might actually be leaving for London with virtue and dignity intact, as evidenced by this scene from the next book in this series:

They stood transfixed, as if frozen in a tableau at the parish church, only they were standing in the doorway of the music room at Weatherby Hall and not believing what they were seeing.

Holly was sprawled on her back on the chaise lounge, her gown pushed up above her knees, the dancing master kneeling between her legs, his pantaloons lowered, along with his smalls, to his knees.o

Lady Mary had her hands up to her mouth, Lily looked like she was going to burst into tears at any moment, and Sir Richard's face depicted his desire to rip the man apart limb by limb.

Glancing up at the family members standing in the doorway, the dancing master flinched. "She is ruined!" he spat out. "We will be wed immediately."

Jane stood with arms crossed and glared stonily at the man. "You will remove yourself forthwith," she declared in a strong, measured tone that brooked no argument. Silence reigned from that moment.

Holly knew her future would be determined then and there. What will it be?

HOUSE OF THE RISING SON

By Trevann Rogers

Music brings them together. Will family tear them apart?

Cheyenne is a half-human incubus whose star is on the rise in the Unakite City rock scene. Obscuring his identity is the only way to keep his kids—the first incubi children born in decades—out of the clutches of the royal family—his family.

Alexander's future is all set—finish law school, join the family firm, and marry someone who'd be good for business. Not that he has a say in any of it. He's barely met the woman his father expects him to marry. Keeping the peace is his priority. Until he meets Cheyenne.

One thwarts his family's savage plan by denying who he is. The other keeps his family placated by hiding who he wants.

If they risk their truths, can they save Cheyenne's children, together?

House of the Rising Son is the first book in the LGBTQIA+ urban fantasy series Living After Midnight.

Warning: This book features quirky supernatural creatures, a Thanksgiving dinner that makes the Inquisition look like a tea party, and an incubus that will rock your world.

The Pumpkin Patch
Bed & Breakfast

www.pumpkinpatchbnb.com

6 South Main Street
Rochester, VT 05767
(802) 767-4742

About The Author

Helene Wallis

Barbara Wallis Felgate is best known for her non-fiction writing, especially her prize-winning essay, "A Day at the Circus (Fire)", about the Barnum & Bailey Circus fire in Hartford, CT in 1944. A link to an interview on YouTube®, in which she reads the essay in full, can be found on her website dedicated to this tragic event, www.1944hartfordcircusfire.com,

A lover of Regency romance, she has now written a debut Regency novella under the name Helene Wallis.

She is currently a charter member and President of Charter Oak Readers & Writers (CORW), a member of (Connecticut Authors and Publishers (CAPA), a member of New England Romance Writers (NERW), and is also a volunteer in her community.

Barbara is a Registered Nurse and the mother of six adult children and ten grandchildren. She is also a volunteer in her community.

She is presently working on several novellas and novels and plans to publish again in 2024. Information about current and upcoming books will be available at www.eklundpublishers.com. She can be contacted at helenewallis@yahoo.com.

Made in United States
North Haven, CT
18 August 2024

Barbara Wallis Felgate was five years old on the day her parents took her to see the circus in Hartford. The date was July 6, 1944. It was a day she and many others would never forget. It was the day the circus tent burned down, killing and maiming hundreds of circus visitors.

Barbara tells her story in an essay "A Day at the Circus (Fire) on YouTube (Zita Christian's Page One podcast – Hartford Circus Fire by Barbara Wallis). There she is interviewed and the story of that event is discussed. Barbara's website about that day is www.1944HartfordCircusFire.com. She can be reached at bfelgate@yahoo.com or 860-916-8887 (you can text a return number). Barbara wants to hear YOUR story about that day. She has written a book, "Sir Richard Meets his Match" as Helene Wallis.